SUPERMOM BREAKS A NAIL

Supermom Breaks a Nail

Kristen Thomas Easley

Copyright © 2010 by Kristen Thomas Easley.

Library of Congress Control Number:		2010917168
ISBN:	Hardcover	978-1-4568-1923-1
	Softcover	978-1-4568-1919-4
	Ebook	978-1-4568-1924-8

All rights reserved. No part of this book may be reproduced or transmitted in any form or by any means, electronic or mechanical, including photocopying, recording, or by any information storage and retrieval system, without permission in writing from the copyright owner.

This is a work of fiction. Names, characters, places and incidents either are the product of the author's imagination or are used fictitiously, and any resemblance to any actual persons, living or dead, events, or locales is entirely coincidental.

This book was printed in the United States of America.

To order additional copies of this book, contact:
Xlibris Corporation
1-888-795-4274
www.Xlibris.com
Orders@Xlibris.com

To Shannon and Maggie,

I love you very much.

I hear you are taking notes for your own book about your Dearest Mommie.

Chapter One

Once Upon a Tuesday

I wake to a sharp pain and Space Commander Joe declaring me an intruder. I sit bolt upright in bed. I turn to see the Space Commander glaring at me from behind a scratched helmet visor. A knot on my forehead forms. My lips curl back to expose most of my gums. "Logan!" I growl to the tussle-haired gremlin behind the action figure.

"Did that hurt, Mom?"

"Yes!" I hiss.

"Huh." He says, quizzically looking at his plastic doll —"Joe didn't even break. He's SUPER STRONG!"—and buzzes out of the room, making whooshing space commander sounds.

I hear my husband groan.

"Heck of a way to wake up, huh?" I say, still trying to rub the pain from my left lobe.

"I didn't wake up until you barked at Logan," he says, rolling over.

Sorry my concussion disturbed your slumber, darling. Coffee?

Since I am up anyway, I collect my "Family Organizer Binder," my "Kiddie Kalendar Spiral," my "Mommy's Portable Memory Book" and my "Keepin' It Together Folder" and head out to the computer. I switch it on and wait, pen poised. The computer comes to life, assaulting me with reminders of the tasks, appointments and activities I have lined up for today. While mapping a course for pick-ups, drop-offs and bank stops, my children remind me they need breakfast. I slap two frozen waffles in the toaster and nuke some day-old coffee in the microwave for myself. With the kids at the table covered in syrup but eating contentedly, I check the clock to see if I have time for a shower. Looks like another day of talcum and air freshener.

After breakfast, I wrestle the kids into outfits that do not match but cover all the parts that should be covered. As my husband is walking out the door, I race by and plant a kiss on him with such force I worry that I've chipped a tooth. Unfortunately, the force of the kiss is not produced from passion but by the fact that I was mid-stumble, having tripped over a four-inch-tall truck left in the middle of the floor. The kids are chewing on their toothbrushes, which seems good enough hygiene to me. I load the two kids and the twelve toys they each need to bring into the car. Getting in the driver's side, I buckle up, sit back, sigh and think to myself, "What the hell happened to me?"

I don't mean to sound ungrateful. I am blessed to have children. At least that is what they tell me—that I am blessed. They say children are blessings and that I should count my blessings, which are two-two currently very dirty blessings, who look like they may have gotten into my baking mix again. But my life before, my Single-With-Out-Children (henceforth to be referred to as SWOC) life, was blessed in a different way. At least there was *some* semblance of sanity to it.

In my SWOC life, I was a decent example of the female race. I did not have a heroic job, but I was good at the ordinary job I had. I took care of myself. I had friends, friends who had a variety of interests and could discuss myriad topics. I was able to follow a TV series while it aired. I used to love the taste of wine. I don't taste wines now. I drink them, when they are in my hand, but I don't taste them. I used to savor every moment I had with my glass of wine. I would let the velvety liquid roll on my tongue and make a game of how many flavors I could identify. Now the game is to see how much I can throw back before one of my children knocks my glass over.

No mother alive needs to be told that her SWOC life and her life as a mother are different. Single women do not need an explanation either. How many friends have they lost to a runny—nosed toddler's schedule? One by one, those "inseparable girlfriends" drop out of Girls' Night and only show up to lunch with child in tow.

But this is not my story. My story is elsewhere. My story is in the fairy tale of motherhood—or the elusiveness of that fairy tale. Magazines blanket the shelves with bylines proclaiming the "Joys of Motherhood." Celebrities allege that their million-dollar lifestyles are meaningless compared to the profundity of being a mother. Media outlets bombard you with the idea that maternity will supersede any positive feeling you've previously felt. The World of Motherhood became more attractive that Alice's Wonderland, the Vikings' Valhalla or Hilton's Shangri-La. With this conditioning, I entered into motherhood willingly and eagerly. And now I wait. I wait for the utopian feeling to come, the rush of euphoria promised me, the ultimate rapturous payoff to be found as a mother that justifies all of my sacrifices.

The reality is that either I suck at being a mother or being a mother sucks.

Chapter Two

Different Creatures Inhabited My Body

Children are like fall fashions. They are different elements but made to work together. My five-year-old, Logan, is a boy and equipped with all the flaws inherent in those models. He chose not to talk until he darn well felt like it, sending us to all kinds of doctors and therapists who scratched their heads and told us he was a "puzzler." As I was writing the $7,000 check to the neurologist to find out the extent of his "puzzling," Logan pointed to a fire truck parked nearby and said, "That fire truck is yellow. They are usually red. Do the different colors mean different jobs when fighting the fire?" I tore up the check and took Logan out for ice cream. He had saved me several thousand dollars, after all.

My daughter, Tabitha, calls herself a princess. She is not. She is a diva. She is incapable of *walking* into a room. She must sashay or dance or stumble into the center. At the ripe age of three, she has adopted referring to people as "dahr-ling".

People who have briefly met my children furrow their brows and say things like "They are bright, aren't they?" or "They are certainly creative children!" I smile and lower my eyes in thanks of their acknowledgement. And they are these things—if by "bright and creative" you mean "strange and possibly unbalanced." I am no authority on children or mothering or anything pertaining to children or mothering (which begs the questions as to why I am writing about said topics), but even I know my children are odd.

Logan is incapable of taking a decent photograph. He might be outside making amazing chalk drawings or building a nuclear generator and looking angelic as he concentrates. As soon as you produce anything that records images or sounds, he will throw open his eyes and mouth in a cartoonish look of shock and begin to make farting sounds. Then he yells at the top of his lungs and runs into the lens. Whenever we show home movies, our friends pat our hands comfortingly and let us know they know of a good program for him.

For six months, Tabby could not speak unless on her head. Asking her what she wanted for lunch would send her into the living room to grab a throw pillow. With pillow in hand, she would return to the kitchen, upend herself and say "Crackers" through her legs. (We were relieved when we got her to use the pillow. I imagine you can only go to the emergency room with your daughter's head wounds so many times before you end up on a few lists.)

As different as they are, they do work together well. There was the requisite jealousy on Logan's part when Tabby was born and the requisite indifference to Logan on Tabby's part when she was an infant and getting all the attention. As soon as Tabby could grab items, the battles began. We steadied ourselves for years of conflict over who had Dad's slipper first (*why* would come later). Then one day Logan introduced Tabby to the baking mix, and a union was forged. In some weird nonverbal dance that culminated in a thin blanket of white, dusting every exposed surface in my kitchen, their roles in each other's lives were established—rank and file. Logan would orchestrate every nefarious plan he could devise, and Tabby would execute it. If Tabby could not execute it, Logan would and leave Tabby holding the bag.

I have walked in and seen the dining room table upended with my Lladro collection precariously positioned on its edge. A line of condiments are poised at the ready to take out the Lladros. I turn, and there is poor Tabby investigating a bottle of mustard that has been hastily shoved into her hand. I growl to Logan to make himself present. He walks into the room, saying, "Tabby did it"—even though I have not accused him of any crime (well, that part was probably obvious).

We have a long discussion about the possibility of Tabby even being able to physically produce the scene at hand. He insists it was all her and isn't the mustard bottle in her hands evidence enough? Poor Tabby is just sitting there, grinning from ear to ear, pleased as punch that Logan is saying her name.

But as the universe would have it, I am constantly reminded of why this is all worthwhile. I pass by the open doorway in Tabby's room. She wants a book she can't reach. Logan puts his action figures aside and says, "Let me help you, Tabby." Logan is sad because some boy at school has said something hurtful. Tabby offers Logan her Princess Pillow because it always makes her feel better.

At night, after all the bedtime battles and negotiations have subsided and sleep has captured their hardworking minds, I creep into their rooms to look at them. Resting peacefully, their precious fingers wrap around my hand as I take theirs. I whisper my love to them.

As I creep to the door, they respond in a loud whisper of their own, "Mom?"

"Yes?" I query back.

"The pudding in my bed is all over my foot—can I sleep in your bed?"

Chapter Three

Remembering Our Foremothers

When we wed, my husband's mother and my mother were as different as they come. One was West Coast; one was East Coast. One worked her whole life; one stayed home. One was still married to the same man she met in college; one was working on separating herself from husband No. 3. One had been raised all over the world; one moved from the house in which she was raised to the one in which she was married—and so on.

Both are pleasant ladies; both are bright; both have an opinion or two on raising children. As far as I can make out, the only thing they agree on wholeheartedly is that I do not truly know what I am doing. And this one commonality has unified them—unified them into one giant, two-headed, advice-dispensing creature. From the moment I gave birth, my husband and I ceased having a mother each. Now we have—The Mothers.

They like nothing more than to pass on their wisdom. Once, after a particularly challenging day, I asked The Mothers the difference between wisdom and meddling. Their reply was somewhere along the lines of its being as vast a difference as between mothering and what I do.

It is not so much *that* they offer their opinion; it is *how* they do it. Instead of plainly stated advice, I get subtle eyebrow raises, a well-placed "Hmm" or thinly veiled sarcasm. Their *bon mots* include "It is so smart of you to keep all this dust on the floor to try to build up your children's allergy resistance." My favorite is "You know, sometimes when our children got us riled up, we would take a moment to glance out the window; breathe out a deep, soothing breath; and then calmly but sternly remind them that what we are telling them to do is for their own good and not just to be mean." This is usually delivered as I am still wiping the froth of rage from my mouth.

To hear The Mothers tell it, they were nothing but a pillar of grace and calm during our childhood. Whatever challenge they faced, whatever problem arose, they found the sensible, appropriate solution and executed it with aplomb.

The only problem with their story is that we were *there*. Did The Mothers take a deep breath when we, as children, first discovered food coloring—on their imported Persian carpet? Did they calmly explain why we should not cut the pretty flowers out of the $1,200 print they just purchased? Did they merely say "Oops" when we knocked over our third glass of milk at the dinner table? No, I don't believe they did. The only deep breath they blew out the window was to hide their cigarette smoke. And we know full well why they did not have dust on the ground—because they hired Marcella to clean it every week.

So not only am I battling their expected level of excellence, I am being measured by a fairy tale they have created of our own childhood. When my husband and I point out their lapses in perfect parenting, they smile calmly and mention they have *recently* been reminded of their psych courses in college when they learned of transference. I think about transferring some of the stale milk into their coffee in the morning.

I try to point out my good qualities like the fact that I SELFLESSLY stay home to raise my children. Then I remember that argument works better if the house is clean and the children aren't half dressed and playing poker with the credit cards from my wallet. I mention how well I did in college, but that only opens me up for comments about the obvious decline in the state's educational system. Exasperated, I point to the window and laud the beautiful weather. It takes a pretty smart cookie to move somewhere THIS beautiful. The Mothers remind me we are here because of my husband's job. So I do the one thing that I am truly good at, the thing that even The Mothers concede I do better than anyone they know—I pout.

Just to show you what I am talking about, here was the reaction to Logan's first accomplishment in swimming when he was three: He was very excited about swimming a short distance in the pool one day. I called The Mothers so he could tell them all about it. After Logan's elusive and abstract version of the day, I took the phone.

"Hi. He was just really excited and wanted to call you," I explain.

"Yes, we can hear the excitement. We are not exactly sure what he said, however [chuckle]. How are the speech lessons going?"

"Good. He has made a lot of improvements. We are really happy with his speech therapist."

"Funny—in our day parents taught their kids to speak."

"Sure. Great news about the swimming, huh? He goes two times a week now."

"Oh, yes. We remember taking you all to the pool every day, usually around 5:00 A.M."

"Well, Logan is only three."

"Hmm, we started you all at 18 months. We had such hope."

"We are thinking . . . wait, hope for what?"

"Nothing."

Pause. Change subject.

"The weather should be beautiful this weekend. We are thinking about heading out to the beach with the kids," I continue.

"You will need sunscreen."

"We have some."

"What SPF?"

"150."

"We always used 175."

Of course you did. I race to the nearest window at the Y, close my eyes and let loose with those deep breaths. When I finally open my eyes, I notice a lifeguard who had been enjoying his break on the other side of the pane.

"Ma'am, it's 10:00 in the morning. Do I smell alcohol?" he asked.

I reply, "Nope. It's SPF 175."

Chapter Four

The Spare Parent

When I write my husband into my mind's romance novel, I name him Count Nathaniel Bloodgoode. I give him a long, flowing mane of silken, raven hair. He wears a velvet riding coat with a scarf sparsely covering his sinewy muscles. This morning I lay in bed in my best seductive pose, waiting for my husband. The Count walked in with his boxers askew and slightly lower than they should be. He was unshaven but in the unkempt, barfly way—not the sexy, Hollywood way. He was absent mindedly chewing on a toothbrush while reading the paper he held in his right hand. His left hand was scratching the lower part of his back slowly and without any apparent reason. When he finally noticed me, the look on my face had changed from seduction to wondering if he realizes he has a second toothbrush tucked behind his ear. He responded, toothbrush still in mouth, "What?"

In light of this, I will just call him Nate.

Nate and I married as partners—no matter what this world threw at us, we would take it on together. We both wanted and eagerly awaited the arrival of children. When I got pregnant, we celebrated for days. He was in the room when I bore both our children and didn't flinch. Once home from the hospital, we would take turns tending and adoring our bundle of wonder. We teasingly argued over who was hogging the baby. We were united and co-parenting.

After a while, we realized something important: Children are tiring and expensive. Since we were committed to one of us staying home, the other had to work more. So we fell pretty comfortably into the traditional roles of working dad and stay-at-home (to be henceforth referred to as SAH) mother.

I did not foresee Nate being tired and not wanting to assume full parenting duties as soon as he walked in the door. I smile through clenched teeth and tell him, "Sure. Go ahead and unwind a bit before 'rolling up your sleeves.'" The fact that I ripped my sleeves off and chewed on them to stifle my screams should have no bearing on his sleeve thing. After an eternity of waiting for Nate to unwind, which is, in reality, the amount of time it takes him to take off his tie), I pout and ask Nate for help. He usually complies.

But he *also* offers an opinion. This part baffles me. What part of *help* indicates *opinion*? I explain quite plainly, if not pedantically, why all of his ideas will not work. I remind him that he did not give them life so he could not possibly have better ideas than I. I see his mind start to work as he furrows his brow. He looks to his children, who do look a great deal like him, and then back at me.

I see his statement forming and beat him to the punch, "Oh, sure, you were involved in the conception," I say, "but having carried two children, I am revoking your right to say you gave them life. *I* gave them life. *I* carried them; *I* birthed them; *I* fed them until my breasts bled—the claim of life is mine. You want to dispute it? Let's shove the dog up your urethra and check back in ten months."

I found, as the children get older, that keeping a handle on them, the house, the chores and any semblance of self-image is getting harder to maintain. On occasion, Nate will come home, and the house is a disaster. He will simply inquire as to what happened and accept my sigh with a hand pointing to the children as an answer. On other nights he will walk in, and the house is a disaster—but now the cat is wearing a tutu; the dog is cowering under the sofa; and I am sitting on a chair, staring at a Korean news TV station (I don't speak Korean). The children are *absent*. He sighs, grabs a beer and a takeout menu.

After the furniture is righted and the light bulbs replaced, Nate will ask me if maybe I need help.

"What do you mean?" I ask incredulous.

"You know, like, maybe a cleaning lady or a babysitter to come by once a week to watch the kids during the day."

"Are you implying I cannot do this?"

"No. I just think you do so much. I am not sure you need to do it all. I hate to see you so work hard."

At this point I would usually call one of my two best friends, but Nate would hear me complaining and perhaps embellishing some of the details of what he had just said. Since I do not need him interfering with my side of the story, I burst into tears and run out of the room and into the arms of the Mommyverse.

(*The Mommyverse is discussed in detail later. A brief description is it is the ever-growing universe of Moms through internet, books, television, support groups and any other form of media that reaches a mom's life.*)

I ask the Mommyverse what they would do if their ungrateful husband called them lazy and fat and unfit to mother his children as mine just had (perhaps I was paraphrasing). The Mommyverse comes back with a resounding cry—if he thinks this is so easy, why not let him stay home with the kids all day and see how well he does? It's a perfect plan. After a day of running after our children, Nate will fall to his knees as I enter the door. He will proclaim his unwavering admiration for how hard I work each day. He will devote his life to finding new ways to appreciate me.

The next morning I casually tell Nate that I am making plans to go up and see a friend in another city on Saturday and could he watch the children? He says, sure, he would love to. Come Saturday, I pack up and head out with a kiss to all. The children are confused but relatively unfazed by my leaving without them.

Twenty minutes into my drive, Nate calls. "Do we have more apple juice?"

I tell him where it is. He tells me to have fun and thanks for the information.

Ten minutes after that, Nate calls again. "Sorry. There is nothing I can't feed them now; right?" he asks. I ask him what he means. "Well, I remember we had to be careful about apples and honey and fish and peanuts at some point in their infancy but no longer; right?"

Hmm, I didn't know he was paying attention. I tell him the kids are fine with all foods. He thanks me, apologizes for bothering me and tells me to have a lot of fun and not to worry about them.

I have a delightful visit, but sometime after lunch I realize that I have not heard from Nate since the car ride up. I picture the house in flames and my children lying on the EMT gurneys, uttering "Mom" with their last breath. I excuse myself outside and call our home number. Nate picks up on the first ring in a hushed voice. I assume he is in the ER.

"What's going on? Where are you?" I ask pointedly.

"I am home, where you called me," he says quietly.

"Why are you whispering?"

"The kids are both asleep."

"They're asleep? Both of them? Logan doesn't nap anymore." I am confused. Did he get them drunk? On purpose?

"I know. But they are both out. Don't worry. I won't let them sleep too long so they go to bed on time. Are you having fun?"

"Oh, yes, we are having a great time. What have you guys been doing?"

"Don't you worry about us," Nate says. "This is your day. You just have fun. I love you."

A terrible feeling nagged me the rest of my visit.

I return home at 5:30 as agreed. When I walk in, the house is seemingly in order. The freshly bathed, pajama'd kids rush me at the door. They excitedly talk of picnics in the backyard, sliding on trash bags wetted by the hose and exciting new heroes Dad had invented. Nate comes from the kitchen followed by a delightful aroma. He kisses me on the cheek and asks if I am hungry. Turns out, he had rediscovered a love for cooking while I was away.

After dinner, Nate declares he will put the kids to bed because he has promised to finish the tale of "Masked Avenging Rodent" they created this afternoon. When he finishes, he joins me in the living room.

"I am so glad you got the day off," he says, taking my hand in his. "And thank you. This was a lot of fun for me."

I burst into tears and run out of the room and into the arms of the Mommyverse.

Chapter Five

Till Momdom Do We Part

In every mother's life lurks that one person she dreads most—the Exceptional Mom. This is the mom who shows up everywhere on time with her children completely dressed (including *both* shoes). She makes breakfast, lunch and dinner at home. She can come up with craft ideas off the top of her head, and those completed crafts are usually museum quality. This mom is the one who actually *bakes* her bake sale item. She can tell you any and all kid-friendly activities within a 50-mile radius. She is the mom who catches all the random items her kids put in her grocery basket *before* she unwittingly brings them home. She has a fairly uniform life even with the children at home. She is basically annoying.

She is also one of my two closest friends. This should put a great deal of pressure on me. However, the other of the two is the antithesis of the Exceptional Mom—the "You're Not Supposed to Do That" Mom; and that balances it all out.

I was one of three gal pals in college—Gigi, Dawn and myself. After college, we settled in different towns, but our bond was intact. We were the Three Musketeers as written by Danielle Steele. We went to college, married, moved and had our babies within months of each other. It was as if we linked our life's timelines together in some cosmic computer program so that we hit every milestone together.

We all came to the decision to stay home with our children independently. Gigi stayed home because her mother strongly suggested it was the only way to properly raise a child, and Gigi is one of the most nonconfrontational people I know. I stayed home to raise my son because at the salary I was making, full-time childcare would have meant I was paying to work at my job. Dawn had not decided what to do by the time she was in her sixth month of pregnancy. One day, she got pissed off at her boss and quit. She told him that she was leaving to stay home and raise her child, which would be far more rewarding than working for him. That last one sends us into gales of laughter every time. More rewarding? Oh, that Dawn—what a cutup!

Since having kids, Dawn and I have had trouble measuring up to Gigi. Her house smells of lemony cleaning products and has an immaculate floor. Her shelves are lined with intellectually stimulating books and photos from their international journeys (*with* her children). Her dishes and cooking equipment are clean and put away in their proper places.

In my house, cooking pots litter the backyard, and most of my silverware has been piled into the dog's water dish. To hide the stains and spills on my floor, I allow my family to disrobe and leave whatever has been removed to lie exactly where it falls. This ensures that I will never find two shoes that match in a 30-minute period. Dawn hired a nanny named Selma to help with the house and kids.

Gigi is perfect, but she is also short. By "short," I mean that someone can rest a drink on her head at parties. I mention this only because it makes me feel better.

Gigi installed a complex but subtle alarm system that alerts the CIA if any unauthorized visitor is anywhere on the property. My alarm system is my children leaving their toys scattered about the floor. Things with bright flashing lights accompanied by shrill sounds are kept in the hallways. This way an adult attempting to relieve themselves in the middle of the night will step on something the whole neighborhood can hear. If we are super lucky, the sound from the toy will set the dog off. Dawn refuses to spend the money on an alarm system. She claims her bag is packed and, if anyone breaks in, she is going to beg them to take her with them anyway.

I came home today and had two messages on the answering machine: one from Dawn and one from Gigi. Given how much I did not accomplish today, I decide to call Dawn first. Comparing myself to Gigi right now might push me over the edge.

"Hey," I say when Dawn answers.

"So you or me first?" she asks.

"You. I need to feel better about myself."

"Sorry to disappoint, but the twins were great today, and I finally got around to making that felt board with the story characters I have been talking about."

"Really?!" I say with a start.

"No," she says laughing. "I stubbed my toe on one of their trucks they had left out and it put me in such a bad mood that I ignored them all day. I tried to get Selma to ignore them too, but she never listens to anything I say. I think I'll fire her."

"Good. Then you can raise your own kids."

We both laugh at the thought of Dawn raising her own kids.

Dawn continues, "Did the Shrimp call you today?'

"Yes, I just heard her message—is something up?" I ask.

"I dunno. I left her a message. No call back yet."

"I was going to call her next—you want to go first."

"Yeah, let me . . . Hey! Uhm . . . you . . . which one are you . . . no, not you . . . your brother . . . SELMA! One of the twins has the mini-vac again . . ."

"Dawn?"

"I should probably be involved in this. Why don't you call Gigi. Let me know what she says."

"I am sure one of her well-behaved children saved the world, and she needle-pointed the story of how they did it to hang in the hallway as kind of a Bayeux Sampler."

"In that case, save it until tomorrow . . . NO! Not the cat! SELMA!"

I reach for the pizza delivery menu, but my hand accidentally grabs an open bottle of Chardonnay instead. I call Gigi.

"Hello?" she answers.

"Hey, Gigi. It's me."

"Oh, thank you for calling back. Thank both you and Dawn for calling me back." Gigi says with relief. Her tone is less chipper than usual.

"What's going on?" I continue.

"Oh, my mother dropped by for a visit today."

"Oh." I say. "How nice?"

"Yes, well, of course it's always great for Sonnet and Schubert to see their grandmother."

"How are you, Gigi?"

"It's hard, having her here. She was just always so . . . perfect as a mother. I am not sure she understands that not all of us are."

My mouthful of chardonnay sprays out of my mouth with a cough. "Us?!" I ask.

"No, I don't mean that you aren't perfect. You are. It is just that you and Dawn see me for who I am—a regular person. You don't care about my flaws." Gigi says with a catch in her voice.

Flaws? Gigi? Surely I misheard. Maybe she said "awes" except that Gigi usually makes sense when she talks.

"Gigi, to us, you are perfect. Regardless."

"That's why I love you guys. Thank you. I feel better. I knew I would. You guys are my salvation," she says with a sigh. "Listen. Sonnet is attempting to cook dinner. I need to go turn the oven on for her. Thank you. I love you."

"I love you too. So does Dawn. She will call you as soon as she bails her twins out of jail."

She laughs. We hang up.

I look to Logan, who is covered in tape and smacking a wooden spoon on the tomato sauce can. I think of Sonnet cooking and sigh. Then I think of Gigi trying to measure up to her mother. I guess we all have an Exceptional Mom in our lives.

Chapter Six

Lying on the Couch

I have a therapist. I see him on a regular basis. I call him even more. He is a wonderful man, very calming and understanding. He always knows just what to say to help me out of a crisis. Just the other day, I called him to tell him I couldn't take it anymore. I was so tired, and nobody appreciated me, not like him at least. If it weren't for my selfless devotion to the betterment of my family, I would cash it all in for a hut in Tahiti. He told me to relax, that many moms have this feeling. He said it was our unending devotion to our families that held everything together. He went on to say that our families would be lost without us. I breathed a heavy sigh of relief—this was all I needed to hear. *"Thank you, Doctor, and since I have you on the phone, could I change Logan's five-year—old check up to the end of the month?"* He connected me with his receptionist.

You see, our pediatrician (to whom I refer as Dr. Godsend) has been our kids' doctor since Logan was six months old. I did not know that I was supposed to have a pediatrician when I had a baby. I knew babies had them; I just thought you got one in the take-home kit the hospital gave you. As I lay on the table after Logan was taken from me, I heard one of the nurses ask for a pediatrician's name. There was a silence. All eyes were on me. Sure they were going to fire me from Momdom before I even got out of the stirrups; I said the name of the pediatrician I had seen growing up in Seattle. They looked from doctor to nurse and back at me. I got panicky and gave them a character's name from the TV series *Rouge Doctors, Inc.*

What do they do to derelict mothers who don't get pediatricians for their babies? Would I not be given my kid until I found one? As I started to cry for the fourth time since giving birth (fifteen minutes now), my OB yelled out a name. The doctor Logan was assigned retired five months after I had my baby.

So twice in six months, my fledgling son was without proper medical care, and I had nowhere to turn. I called Gigi to confer. She called some moms she knew in my area, and they all said they LOVED their pediatrician, Dr. Godsend. But he was not taking any new patients. It turns out, if you sit on a pediatrician's doorstep and sob with your screaming newborn long enough, they will take you on as a patient. You just need to know the system.

I think Nate is jealous of Dr. Godsend. Part of the problem may be I use the term "Godsend" in reference to our pediatrician and not my husband. I come home from Dr. Godsend's office and say how *wonderful* he is with the children and how he can *exactly* read my feelings. I tell Nate how Dr. Godsend knows just the right thing to say to make me feel better. He *really* listens to me. We had a slight disagreement over our holiday gift to Dr. Godsend. Nate suggested I make a donation in Dr. Godsend's name to a charity he supports. I, in turn, went out and bought him a new car. Well, I tried, but dealerships don't take airline miles as payment. Either way I was justified, and here's an example:

My anxiety attacks started coming regularly when Logan was three and started going to preschool. *I* thought Logan was an active but generally sweet little boy, who had yet to find his volume button. *The preschool* saw him as an unruly hellion who could not follow instructions. They complained that Logan refused to sit passively for 20 minutes after a carbohydrate-laden snack. I complained that my husband was the same way. They were not amused. They pointed out that Logan had a peculiar habit of running during "outside play." I was stumped since that is what I thought they were supposed to do during "outside play." Clearly I had my work cut out for me.

Every day I would receive that look—the one the teacher gives you that tells you she needs to speak with you about your child. I would go over and ask, "How was he?" bracing myself for the answer. A toy was thrown, sand flew, squiggling took place, pushing, not putting toys away—you name it. Whatever the offense could be, my little Logan committed it. As the "How to Raise a Kid" books suggest, I discussed Logan's behavior with him in very calm, soothing tones. I did not imply that anyone thought he was wrong but perhaps he could rethink his actions so that he could form more loving relationships with those around him. When the discussion did not produce any significant change, I deprived him of sweets and TV. I sat with Logan and watched countless hours of video on how to be a good little boy (though all little boys are special, they said).

I called Gigi and Dawn about my miscreant's behavior, but they played the supportive friends and did not really give me any direction. In a moment of poor judgment, I broke down and called The Mothers. I whimpered into the phone that clearly something had gone terribly wrong with one of the strands of DNA (probably Nate's) and my child was destined to end up in jail by high school. I carefully recounted the endless offenses committed. As usual, The

Mothers had their far out, archaic beliefs that followed the general thoughts of "He sounds like a little boy to me." Obviously I had only one resource, I made an appointment with Dr. Godsend.

I forced Nate to stay with our daughter so I could give this situation proper attention. Logan and I went to the office and sat in our colorful plastic molded seats. I rested my head against the wall behind me and looked at the ceiling, wondering if God was going to get around to my repeated asking of "Why me?" Logan found some books and started reading. I see now that his was a more productive use of time. Something in the book tickled him, and he began to laugh. By the time Dr. Godsend came in, Logan was laughing uproariously at some dog splashing in a puddle. I threw my hand out in his direction and looked at the doctor as if to say "See?!?"

"What's the problem?" Dr. Godsend asked.

I went on to chronicle the last nine years of my life which included marrying; birthing children; giving up my career and, it seems, all claims a normal life. To be helpful, I peppered the story with my own theories about certain behaviors and where they came from (probably Nate). At the end I was emotionally spent. I steeled myself for the barrage of questions about to come that would be used to judge my son's mental state. Dr. Godsend started:

"So he is active?"

"Yes"

"Loud?"

"Very"

"Runs around when he should be sitting?"

"All the time."

"Doesn't want to do what he is told unless threatened with repercussions?"

"Never."

"Pushes the boundaries to see what he can get away with?"

"Constantly."

It's like he was reading my mind.

Dr. Godsend regarded his notes and cocked an eyebrow.

"Wh-what is it?" I asked with great trepidation.

He took a deep breath and said, "There's good news and bad news."

"What's the good news?" I asked, relishing the possible shimmer of hope.

"I have seen this before."

"And what is it?" I asked anxiously.

"Your son is a three-year-old little boy," he said.

I gasped. "What's the bad news?"

"It gets worse."

"HOW?!?"

"Adolescence."
"Is there anything you can prescribe for it?"
"Valium"
"For a three-year-old?"
"For you."

I don't care what Nate says. Next Christmas I am getting Dr. Godsend a summer home.

Chapter Seven

You Light Up My Life

After you select your spouse, the second most important person you select is your babysitter. I knew I was supposed to be very concerned about who would watch my baby. Their ability to discern a choking child from a giggling one should have been paramount in my thoughts. All I could really think of was: NIGHT OUT.

Soon after Logan was born, I was given a recommendation for a sitter. Since the woman who gave me the name seemed generally concerned with her child's well-being, I went with her recommendation. I called the sitter, told her how I had come by her name and could she babysit? I was not prepared for:

The interview.

Let me introduce this fact now—childrearing today is more about interviews than anything else. You interview anyone involved in your child's life. Worse, you are interviewed at every interview as well. So is your child. Childrearing is fraught with potential rejection.

For the interview with our prospective babysitter, I had a professional cleaning crew come in to steam clean the house. I kept trying to slip them 20s to zap the kid, but they weren't going for it. I spent the days leading up to the interview selecting an outfit. I contemplated a dress for a "Donna Reed" type impression, but my dresses give more of a "Cher" impression. I settled on an old bridesmaid dress from the 80s—heck, let her think we were fancy. I bought scones from the store that were rock hard by the time of the interview. I became obsessed with the look of Nate's hair. I made him brush it five different ways before the sitter arrived. Poor Logan, who was only three months old at the time, was changed repeatedly into different outfits, each one getting increasingly more Victorian in its appearance. Finally she arrived:

Mary Poppins.

Okay. Her last name is not really Poppins, but I am not revealing her last name. You might live in my area and need a sitter.

I swear she had a heavenly glow surrounding her when I opened the door. Nate says it was just a sun glare off of a Chevy across the street. We drank tepid tea and gnawed on scones as we exchanged pleasantries. Then there was a pause. We smiled and looked at one another. Finally Mary leaned in and asked, "Is there anything you would like to ask me?"

I raised my eyebrows and glanced at Nate. "Uhm . . . ask you?"

"Yes, about my experience or philosophy or . . . child-raising things?"

I honestly hadn't thought this was about *us* interviewing *her*. But as soon as she said it, it seemed like such a good idea. She was brilliant and I loved her.

"How much do you charge?" asked Nate.

She told us.

Once we were able to breathe again, we tried to think of some other questions.

"I am curious, Just from a Humanist's point of view, what do other families ask you?" I ventured.

"Well, some like to know how I discipline. Some like to know what I am certified in."

"You mean like martial arts?"

"No, more along the lines of CPR, first aid, that type of thing."

"That, oh—of course, those would be good things to know." I said, losing hope of ever seeing her again.

Mary asked if she could hold Logan, who had been quite fussy through the whole event. Upon reaching her arms, he laid his little head on her shoulder and promptly fell asleep. He smiled as he breathed heavy sleep breaths. I began to wonder if he liked her better. Eventually we placed Logan in his crib, led Mary to the door and shook her hand. I knew it was appropriate to wait three days, but I couldn't. I needed to know right now.

"So do you think you might have room in your schedule to sit for us on occasion?" I asked expectantly.

Mercifully, she said "I think we can arrange something."

When she had left, I picked up the phone and started dialing. Nate asked what was going on.

"I am applying for a line of credit."

"Is that necessary?" he asked.

"I'm not taking any chances."

"She did seem competent."

I looked at Nate and smiled a wide smile. "Do you know understand what this will mean for us?" I asked wistfully.

"I do." he said, returning my smile.
We both said our answers at the same time:
"Movie night" I said.
He said, "Sex."
Tomato, Toe-mah-toe.

Chapter Eight

What the Blog?

I was not prepared for the amount of questions I would have when I first had children. "Wait. Why is it doing that?" became my mantra. I asked The Mothers how they answered these questions when they were new moms. Their form of networking was a letter to their mother or a phone call to a sister. They told me to rely on common sense and gut instinct. Dismissing these addled-minded adages, I called Dr. Godsend. He said he did not like to diagnose over the phone and that, although he was sure Logan did produce an odd-pitched wail while yawning, my attempt to duplicate it wouldn't help find out what caused it. He suggested I expand my avenues for finding answers—perhaps to consult a couple of blogs. I agreed and conferred with my "How to Raise a Kid" books to find out what a blog was. This is how I discovered the Mommyverse.

The Mommyverse is a cyber-world for moms filled with advice, counseling and proverbial shoulders to cry on. At first, I thought I would consult the Mommyverse only occasionally. But after I found an army of like-minded, tormented and misunderstood moms, I couldn't stay away. Not only can they tell me the best way to dislodge a block from my child's nose, they confirm that Nate is completely wrong—regardless of what he's done. I get sympathy when I decry The Mothers' outdated theories about discipline (like actually doing it). I am omnipotent—and finally not just in my own head. What started out as a mild fascination quickly turned into an addiction.

In the beginning, I had trouble deciphering Mommyverse speak. I tried to find some kind of Mommyverse dictionary, but there wasn't one. My sister-in-law decoded some of the acronyms for me. People in the Mommyverse refer to their children as DD and DS. The first initial stands for "Darling" or "Dear" and the second initial stands for "daughter" or "son." I thought, "these people must really adore their children. I wished I liked my kids that much."

But then I read sentences like "my D(darling)S(son) flushed the cat down the toilet while my D(dear)D(daughter) painted the kitchen floor in Jell-O" and realized I was home. As for a husbands, I read "My D(dearest)H(husband) and I were at it again last night." I think I am going to read about some juicy bedroom antics. But the Mommyverse blogger will go on to say, "DH is an idiot who has no idea how to raise a child and is generally undermining me as a person." Ah, she called him "Dearest"—how sweet.

Gigi asked why we use such euphemisms in which to couch our anger. I tell her I certainly don't want *Sassyknitter38* judging my family. She wondered if maybe the best way not to be judged would be to not tell the Mommyverse, in the first place. What does Gigi know? She's short.

If I work myself into a proper dither, I can be lost to the Mommyverse for hours. Once I lodge my complaint, I sit back wait for the responses. Hundreds of my Momhood sisters vindicate me. I rise from my chair through no force of my own but on the shoulders of my fellow moms. I float into the living room, deposit a take-out menu on Nate's lap and pour myself another glass of wine.

Like all addictions, I was forced to examine my behavior. For me, the bend in the road came with "The Battle of *DaphneDoesIt* and *WunderTwinsMummikins.*" It began when *WunderTwinsMummikins* blogged how upset she was by an incident that had happened at a park. Her post chronicled how she deposited her kids on a play structure and went off to talk to her friends. Shortly thereafter, a red-faced fellow park mom came up to *WunderTwinsMummikins* with one of *WTM's* children in tow.

This child had apparently staged a mutiny of the playground and cut a sandy swath of startled children in his wake. The Park Mom was pretty pissed and told *WunderTwinsMummikins* what she thought of *WTM's* parenting. *WunderTwinsMummikins* cried to the Mommyverse as soon as she got home. What had she done wrong? How can she be expected to dissect the latest reality show's reject with her friends AND watch her children at the same time? Why had this other mom been so mean? The Mommyverse took the Park Mom to task. Who was this bitch? How dare she *physically* remove *WTM's* child from beating her own?

DaphneDoesIt ventured to ask if maybe *WunderTwinsMummikins* could have done more to manage her children in public. *DaphneDoesIt* was the first time I witnessed a cyber-sacrifice. She was devoured and not heard from again. Sometimes I still wonder whether it was *that* she challenged or *how* she challenged. Did she deserve expulsion, and where had she gone for refuge? I wonder . . . but I dare not ask the Mommyverse.

Chapter Nine

In the Club

After "The Battle" on the Mommyverse, I once again cast my net for answers and acceptance in the world of mothers. My "How to Raise a Kid" books said to join a moms' club; so I did.

A Moms' Club is a support group. You attend weekly meetings with mothers, who all have children around the same age, and discuss being a mom. Usually there is a leader who may have an advanced degree in child psychology or maybe just "really, really loves kids and being a mommy!" Unlike the Mommyverse, in a Mom's Club I was surrounded by live moms who made sad faces and touched my shoulder. They told me how what I said is just like their own experience. Then they proceeded to tell me *their* story . . . for 20 minutes. I was a new mom. I could make sad faces. And now I had mom stories. I belonged.

This is how I joined the Judgmental Moms' Club. We did nothing but discuss our children's development . . . and by "development," I mean "What my child can do and yours can't." We compared various philosophies to childrearing . . . and by "compare," I mean we said mean spirited things about the women who did things differently. We condemned television for our child's malleable minds—well, unless we absolutely needed to get something done or to get a moment to ourselves or we were talking on the phone or to settle them down for bed or because we were exhausted or our soaps were on or . . .

We proclaimed proudly that WE knew what was best for our baby and that our mothers and sisters and grandmothers were clueless. I was wading in the pool of popularity, and all it had taken was ten months gestation and a few stretch marks. It didn't take long for the cracks in the foundation of the JMC to form. The first was when we discussed sleeping through the night. Dawn warned me about offering up this information. But one day we were asked to go around the room, tell how long your baby slept and what was working or not working. We were not supposed to speak until we had the Time-to-Talk Teddy Bear passed to us. It was a rule. When the Time-to-Talk Teddy Bear came my way, I told the group "eight hours." There were a gasps and a few glares.

"Wow. What is working?" Dr. Misty, our 23-year-old-just-earned-her-PhD leader asked.

"Uhm, I am not sure. He just kind of started sleeping longer." More glares.

"Really? Nothing different in your routine?"

"No, I don't think so. I mean, you know, he's changing, you know, developmentally but nothing more than what the books say," I said cautiously looking around.

"When is your last feeding at night?" Dr. Misty asked.

"Oh, uhm, I think . . ."

A particularly vocal member of the group cut me off. "*What* are you feeding him?" she snarled.

I sputtered "Oh, uhm, well, you see, he was an early teether so he bit a lot and I had to . . . well, it hurt quite a bit . . ."

"Formula," she sneered.

A collective cluck came from the group. The Time-to-Talk Teddy Bear was taken from my lap, and my views on sleeping were not requested again.

Once we were talking about sitters. Most of the moms were working up the effort to have their first sitter (although several had had their babies in daycare since they were three months old). Some were even contemplating if they could trust their own parents to watch their children. I was not asked much for my opinion these days. However, I kept trying.

On some level, I believed that, if the JMC rejected me, it would be noted in some giant Unfit Mothers ledger that existed somewhere. So I offered up what I thought would be helpful for some to hear. "I have had a wonderful sitter for Logan since he was only a few months old."

"How long had you known your sitter before she sat for you?" Dr. Misty asked.

"Oh, we met once, you know, at the interview, and then I think she came over that next week to sit. It was wonderful."

"Were you in the house?" one mom asked.

"When?" I asked.

"During the first time she sat." she said.

"I was . . . out at a restaurant." I replied.

The group gasped.

"Oh, my, no! You should never leave your children alone with a babysitter the first night. What if something had happened?" someone said.

"But isn't that why she is there? So I don't have to be?" I asked.

"Not the first time!" another barked.

"My sister still hasn't left the baby alone with the sitter, and it's been five months."

"My step-cousin and his wife would sit in the closet while the babysitter was there," someone added. Everyone nodded as if this somehow made sense.

I shrank back and looked nervously at Logan. Seriously, why am I not getting this?

I did not renew my membership once my six weeks were up, and my new support group members did not keep in touch.

I asked The Mothers why their generation did not need all these groups for moms. They said they did, but they called them Stitch and Bitch Clubs. Not only did they solve the world's problems, they usually got a quilt out of it. No one cared if their husbands were co-sharing in parenting. Frankly, the more their husbands were out from underfoot, the smoother their homes ran.

They dispensed advice like "Just put some scotch on it." Alcohol and cigarettes were present, if not the theme of the meeting. Membership was free, and drop-ins were welcome. Beware if you missed an evening, though. You were probably the subject of that night's discussion. Stitch and Bitch's are no longer around. Parenting is serious business now. Any advice written before 1999 is null and void.

Nate suggested I organize my own Moms' Club. Since I needed to meet more women in my area anyway, I took to the Mommyverse. I posted on every site to which I belonged—"Come join other bright moms who refuse to get sucked into today's Parenting Vacuum." Well, that was what I was thinking when I posted. I think I actually wrote something closer to "Anyone want to join a new Mom group on the Westside?" I got a bunch of responses—

"YYYEEESSS!!!!"

"Wow—it's like you were reading my mind!!!"

"I would LOOOOOOOOOVE to join—sing (sic) me up!!!!"

"This comes at just the right time. I was feeling so down on myself lately—you know, like nobody gets me and I keep messing everything up; and now I feel like I have a home, a place to go."

This sounded like a nice gaggle of girls. I wrote a personal message to everyone interested. I explained how I wanted to do something different. I said it was more of a women's group than just a mom's group. I thought we would discuss all kinds of women's issues and we would be free from criticism. Everyone was allowed her opinion as long as no one made it personal. The ladies were enthusiastic. They gave me quite a few words of encouragement with an excess of vowels and exclamation points.

Our first order of business was to introduce ourselves via email and then to set our first meeting. The introduction was easy. I received volumes of emails as these nine ladies divulged every fact about themselves and any thought they had ever had on parenting or marriage or women in general.

Next, we were to set the first meeting. This proved a bit tricky: there were babysitters to obtain, schedules to consider (kids, work, husbands, etc). Once the date was set, we were forced to cancel that first meeting and reschedule 16 times. Finally, four months after my initial posting, we were all set to meet at my house. Light refreshments, wine and no kids—for this first meeting. I sent out my address and phone number for the third time that week. My kids were thrilled to be going to Der Pizza Haus with Nate. They dragged him out the door without saying goodbye.

Two hours before the meeting I received an email from one of the group. She was awfully sorry, but she did not realize how far away I lived. This struck me as odd since it was one of the first things we discussed. Anyway, she would need to bow out, and maybe this is not the time for her in such a group, but it is a great idea and she wished us the best of luck. Once the first excuse was made, the floodgates were opened. The others' excuses ranged from life's current direction taking a different course to self-image issues to pedicure emergencies. My woman's group had dissolved, and we hadn't once met.

In the end, it was me and my 86-year-old neighbor sipping chardonnay as she told me about how she hadn't been able to feel the left side of her tongue in 15 years. When my family returned, Nate pointed to our neighbor who had wet herself while asleep on the couch. I said she was my spirit guide to womanhood and went to bed.

Chapter Ten

Does Oxford Have After School Care?

I read volumes on preschool in my "How to Raise a Kid" books. It seemed like a great idea for a mom. I thought I would get a few hours to myself while some lovely people bettered my children through song and sand play. Getting them into preschool is another story. When I was a part of the Judgmental Mom's Club (Logan and the other babies were six months at the time), our leader Dr. Misty asked if anyone had any news. One mom replied, "My little Dakota Skyye just got in to University of Smarts!" This was met with squeals and congratulations. I wondered, "We were supposed to have signed them up for college already?!?"

Turns out, she was referring to a coveted daycare program.

You can put a baby in daycare as early as you like. Preschool starts when the child is two or two and a half. Where you send them carries as much status as the car you drive. I started looking for a preschool for Logan when he was two. I was told that it would be tough as I started my search too late. By some terrible coincidence, an organization was running ads on TV proclaiming that, if I did not send my kid to preschool, then he would probably not do well in elementary school. This meant he would fail high school. Subsequently, he would never see the inside of a college—and inhabit my basement until he was 45.

Most preschools require your child be potty trained prior to enrolling. If you have yet to actually potty train a child, let me tell you, stress of a deadline is not helpful to the process. If you consult the Mommyverse, they will tell you potty training is taking place later these days. Parents aren't even starting until the child is three. So if kids start preschool at two and potty training should be expected around three and kids had to be potty trained to go to preschool—who was filling up all the preschools and keeping my kids on wait lists?

Luckily, I discovered an alternative to preschool. The public school up the street from me offered pre-kindergarten. Thirty lucky four-year-olds would be enrolled on a first-come, first-served basis.

I asked Dawn about the first-come, first-served part. She said preschool spots were harder to come by than Rolling Stones' tickets. I figured pre-K slots would be the same. The first day of the enrollment period, I got up at 6:45, showered and dressed. My outfit was comfortable but respectable enough to look like a responsible mom. My paperwork was filled out and in order. I grabbed my purse, thermos and book and headed out.

As I rounded the corner, the school came into view. I could make out yellow signs and pylons set up to control the chaos and direct us line sitters. I was relieved to see that there was not a huge line in front of the school. As I got closer, I saw the signs and cones were for student drop-off and not the enrollment at all. Four ladies were chatting outside the school's office. I was thrilled—even if all four ladies were signing up, there would still be slots for me. Now I just had 70 minutes to read my book and drink my coffee.

I entered the office to see if I needed to sign in. One of the two nice ladies from behind the counter asked if she could help me. I said "I am here for the pre-K enrollment. Do we just line up outside?"

As if we were in a movie, all sound immediately ceased. Both ladies behind the desk looked at the clock and then one said, "We don't start until 9:00 A.M."

"Oh, I know. I just . . . ." I looked around and noticed the ladies out front were now gone, having been just moms catching up before school. The school grounds were empty. It was 7:50, and I was there for a 9:00 A.M. enrollment.

"I was afraid there was going to be a big line," I said.

The lady looked at me and again said, "But we don't start until 9:00."

"Uhm, okay. I could come back," I said.

"I could give you a number," she replied, looking around the desk. "But I haven't made them up yet. We don't start enrollment until 9:00."

"Sure. Okay," I said, a bit too high pitched. "Should I come back in a half hour?"

She replied, "Or an hour."

"Great." I said, trying to sound unfazed.

"Well, let me get your name so I know you were here . . . first." The last thing she said was "You have everything; right? I can't enroll you unless you have everything."

Of course I was fully prepared.

An hour later, I started back up to the school. The grounds were quiet now. I walked into the office and smiled at my two new friends. Seeing absolutely nobody else around and 15 minutes left before enrollment began, I took a seat on the bench reserved for students awaiting discipline. I had forgotten my book; so I read all the fliers about programs, school calendars and "What's Hot in the Cafeteria" menus. I chose a book from the selection offered which included such classics as "I Know My Shapes!" (which, apparently, I do). I was very much alone on my detention bench, reading my Scholastic Book. Nobody else showed up for enrollment. The principal came out at one point, glanced at me and asked if I needed help. "Nope. I am fine," I assured her. She looked to the secretaries.

"Enrollment," one said.

"But we don't start until 9:00." the principal said. I tried to hide behind my "Fuzzy Kitty" book, but they just don't make those big enough.

At 9:00 A.M., I was called to the desk. I approached with my neat folder and paperwork all lined up according to the coversheet. She pulled out the first set, a long form that had six carbon pages to it. She reviewed the information on the sheet and then lifted the first set of pages to reveal that it was not six carbon sheets, it was 2x3 sets of carbons. After all this, I was standing there unprepared. She generously allowed me to stand off to the corner to complete them. Filling them out as quickly as I could, I neglected to read the headers and filled out all the "For Office Use Only" sections on the bottom as well—more points for me.

She put me on next year's attendance sheets and I flew out of the office before they could change their minds. Not looking up, I crashed into a lady standing outside of the office.

"Oh, my gosh. I am so sorry!" I said, collecting my scattered papers.

"That's quite all right," she said. "Hey, did you just enroll your child here?"

"Yes, I did. Pre-K."

"Well, welcome to the school!" Her tone had taken on a cheerleader quality. "Do you have your tutors lined up?"

"Tutors? For what?"

"Your child?" she answered.

"The one starting pre-K?"

"Yes."

"No."

"Haven't you seen the new ads on TV?" she gasped.

I called Nate and told him we needed to buy a house with a basement—two basements, actually, at 45 Logan and Tabby shouldn't be sharing a room.

Chapter Eleven

Wanna Go Out?

There are many kinds of dates: dinner dates, blind dates, double dates, movie dates, obligatory dates, set-up dates, repeat dates, "My mother wants us to marry" dates, group dates, "This is not a date" dates, "I can't go see a movie alone" dates, "I have no money. Will you feed me?" dates—you name it. And I have been on many of them. Once I got married, I thought I was through with dating. But then I entered the Era of the Playdate.

When I was little, I popped over to the neighbor's house to see if their kid was home and wanted to play with me. I was offered chips in a bowl and frozen juice boxes that I sucked on until they melted. I don't think we had a fancy name for it. It all seemed kind of simple and fun.

Now it's, well, a "date." One mom calls the other and requests said playdate.

"Hi! How about a playdate? Does Thursday work?"

"Oh, shoot! We have speech therapy. How about Wednesday?"

"Sorry. We have Itty Bitty Belly Dancing."

"Oh! Our Spiritual Enlightenment for Tots is canceled this week; so we can meet for an hour on Friday morning—how's that for you?"

"Uhm, let me check. Yes! We can come over between Petite Polo Lessons and Kiddie Kordon Bleu."

"Great. See you then!"

I gather both my children—everything is done in a group now—and head over to their friends' house at the appointed time. When I arrive, general pleasantries are exchanged, and the next 20 minutes are spent asking our children questions designed to bring them together as a unit.

"Logan? Did you say hello to your friends?"

"Dag? Pippy? Did you see that Logan and Tabby are here? Come out and see your friends. Now, come on. You have been watching TV all morning. Let's turn off the TV and say hi to your friends."

(To me) "They don't usually watch that much TV, but I had to get some housework done."

"Logan, do you want to sit by Dag? Tabby, Pippy got a new doll, isn't that nice? Now, kids, this is somebody else's house. Let's not climb on the furniture. Logan! This is not your house. Get out of the refrigerator."

(To Dag's mom) "He never does this—I don't know what is wrong with him today."

After spending most of our efforts in attempting to get the children we have assembled to interact in a social manner, we break out the big guns—the Activity.

"Since it is so close to Easter, I thought we would do a season-appropriate activity," Dag's mom says. "Of course, we do not want to show a bias to any one denomination; so we are incorporating many elements. We will paint eggs with a scene of Jesus attending a Purim Carnival as Buddha. Won't that be fun?"

The kids' eyes do not leave the TV until they see paint—paint, the Great Unifier. Suddenly four sets of hands have paintbrushes, and "washable" neon paint is flying in every direction but on the egg. Both Dag's mom and I frantically try to save at least one surface from the paint splatters. Then a child drops an egg. It breaks.

Silence.

The children's' eyes grow wide. The Battle of Humpty Dumpty is launched. Eggs are smashed on the table, the floor, each other's heads, the parakeet—you name it. I crouch down and try to pick up tiny bits of shell. I alternate between apologizing for my children and asking them to please decide not to destroy the eggs and their friends' house in the process. Dag's mom repeatedly asks, "Don't you want to paint the pretty eggs? Look what Mommy's doing . . . wow—isn't that beautiful? Isn't this fun, Logan's Mommy? This is much more fun than breaking the poor eggs. Stop crying eggs. We are sorry we are smashing you."

A halt is called to the activity, and the food comes out. Here we have one of two scenarios: The first is that I was counting on my children getting fed lunch so I could successfully avoid my motherly duties for one more meal. Instead Dag's mom serves up some healthy, organic, pasty, non-exploited-worker-type fare my children won't touch, let alone eat. Or the second, I have actually gotten some healthy food in my children, and Dag's mom whips out a sampling of Willy Wonka's factory on a platter. My children cram so much sugar in their mouths that they vibrate for three days.

Dag's mom notes the clock, and so it is time to make our goodbyes. The children have finally decided to interact and are running about the house squealing and having a grand time. Thirty minutes later, I have a screaming child under each arm. I thank Dag's mom for the lovely time. "Let's speak next week when we can arrange for another playdate. What fun this was. Why don't we do this more often?"

Chapter Twelve

Little Bundles of Joy?

Some moms dream of all the time they get to spend with their child. They start pacing during naps because they simply can't wait for the baby to wake up so they can play with him/her. There are moms (and I am fairly confident Gigi is one of them) that honestly believe that every act they do is enhanced by having their children along. I admire these women, but I am not one of them. I am trying to figure out how early any military school will take my children.

I am not trying to suggest that my children are Machiavellian. Yet I must applaud their new and ingenious ways of trying to drive me out of my mind. Today the dog gave me a look that let me know he was none too pleased with me. When he turned around, I noticed he had been colored in various shades of sidewalk chalk and that stickers covered his hindquarters.

Last month the kids and I hosted their aunt and little cousin Erma at our house. I told Logan that I wanted to chat with his aunt; so why did he not play with Erma and Tabitha and let us alone. As we chatted in the living room, we heard the wonderful sound of pleasant play in the other room. There were peals of laughter, shrieks of delight, bursts of joyous noise, the sound of the whipped cream can . . . wait, that's not right. I walked—well, ran, actually—to the other room and saw the worst pancake recipe ever created. On the floor were the contents of my baking mix box, the entirety of the regular and chocolate milk cartons as well as the mustard and some minced garlic. Most of the ingredients had been scooped off the floor and into Nate's shaving mug, which was then ceremoniously thrown in the closet.

The last trip we took up to see my parents, my children were angels in the airport. People took the time to tell me how lovely they were and what a treat it was to watch them interact with each other. I smiled and thanked each well-wisher while wondering to myself "*Why are my children acting so well?*"

Once on the plane, we took our seats. There were only three seats to a row so Nate sat across the aisle from the kids and me. When I attempted to put their seatbelts on, my children reacted as if I was trying to shove frogs into their pants. They launched into a hand war with me as I tried to work the buckle. I turned to Nate for assistance. He shrugged to indicate that he could not get out of his seat due to proper takeoff regulations. I shrugged to indicate there would be no sex for a while. So I tried reasoning with the children. We all know how reasonable young children are on planes.

"Now, now, kids. Remember we are going to see Nana and Bepop. How exciting is that?"

Logan asked where they were. I told him. His cries of subjugation about the seatbelt switched to cries of injustice of grandparent withholding.

"No," I assured him, "we are going to see them really soon. But the pilot cannot leave until your seatbelt is buckled. That is why we are all sitting here—waiting for you."

This is when the plane started to back up. My son looked at me with his familiar "*Have you no shame?*" look. The flight attendant came down the aisle, checking all of us out for proper take off form.

"He will need to have his seatbelt on for takeoff." she said impatiently.

"Ah," I think, "then I should probably discontinue this clever game of Smack Mom's Hands and get on that."

She hovered over me to make sure I completed my task. I got desperate. I held him down with one firm hold and buckled him with the other hand. The volume of his screams was making the fellow passengers' ears bleed. "Stop it!" I said. "Your sister is not making this kind of fuss! Look at her . . ."

Dammit, where was Tabitha? I turn back to Nate, who was inexplicably sleeping.

"Where is Tabitha?!" I demanded, shoving him awake.

"Isn't she with you?" he asked.

"Would I be asking you where she was if that were true?" I hissed through my teeth.

"Hey!" I heard from the seat in front of us. An angry, formerly sleeping gentleman whipped his head around, "Is this your kid?"

As I peered over the seats, I saw a small head of tousled curls grinning up from between the man's legs. His briefcase was open. It appeared as though my daughter had reorganized his report with a few Sharpie notes. I apologized profusely and told him I would be happy to replace anything she damaged. I reached over to extract her from her spot, growing increasingly aware that I was reaching for his crotch. As I awkwardly tried to grab her and not him, he became frustrated and tried to lift her up himself. Her shoe got caught on the tray table. He repeatedly jerked her up to no avail—shaking the seat of the lady in front of him. Finally, my daughter's legs were freed and I took her from him—but not before she got off a solid kick to the head of the man in front of Logan.

Logan? Where was he now? I turned quickly to see Logan on Nate's lap. Nate gave me that look—the one that asks, "*Why you don't have this under control?*" And I give him that look—the one that says, "*I do not care for your opinion at this time.*"

The flight attendant came by and angrily reminded me that everyone needed to be in their seats with their seatbelts buckled. I smiled tightly and put Tabitha in her seat, locking her in. I put Logan in his seat and secured him. I dumped the contents of my purse and the baby bag onto their laps and let them do whatever they wanted with whatever was there. As I fantasized about airline-sized bottles of vodka lined up before me, the children's volume slowly started to rise. I turned to Nate who was, once again, asleep. My children commenced launching my purse items onto the heads of our fellow passengers throughout the plane.

When we arrived, the grandparents were waiting for us. Embraces happened and kisses were administered. My dad could not help noticing the other passengers yanking their luggage from the carousel and glaring at us as they passed by.

"How was the flight?" Dad asked.

"Super!" Logan said. "We got to talk to the pilot."

"You're joking?" Dad asked. "What did he say?"

Logan replied, "He said, 'Stop it!'"

As we headed out of the airport, my father put his arm around me and told me how glad he was we were there. "We have some of your favorite meals planned; your old room is all made up for you, and a fire is laid in the hearth waiting for you. The football game is on at 1:00," he said

"Thanks Dad," I said, leaning into him.

He leaned in closer and whispered, "And I bought the good scotch—lots of it."

I love coming home.

Chapter Thirteen

Crime and Punishment

When it comes to discipline, the "How to Raise a Kid" books imply children today have evolved with functioning and logical minds by the time they are nine months old. We no longer need the barbaric ways of our predecessors that involve angered tones or stern language. Instead, we can have a loving and open discourse with our children, which allows them a say in a situation. Many times their inappropriate behavior (we do not use 'bad' as a modifier as it implies the child is flawed) is a result of their frustration about not having an equal voice in the rules and workings of the household. If you simply allow the children the opportunity to make the right decision, they will.

I have found a small flaw in this theory when it comes to my children. If I allow them the opportunity to make the right decision, they will consistently and categorically make the decision to do what they want with little to no regard for what the correct decision is. After a few years of having every boundary I ever set smashed, I decided *perhaps* we could attempt some form of discipline. I was tired of apologizing to every person we encountered for the action/word/sound my children made.

I decided to try the "How to Raise a Kid" books' recommendation and have a comprehensive discussion with my children about their actions. I needed to clearly lay out what is expected of them. I could do this. I had negotiated contracts in my former SWOC life. I had been asked to write papers arguing my points in college. Surely I could engage in constructive discourse with my children about my expectations.

Fortunately, I was provided the opportunity to try this approach out almost as soon as I had made the decision to try it. Tabitha knocked down Logan's block tower one too many times. She pushed the tower, and he pushed her.

Unfortunately, given her natural balance, she toppled over. She screamed, and he immediately went on the defense. I sent him to his room to think about his actions. After an appropriate amount of time, I called Logan to the living room. I sat him next to me on the couch. In the calmest voice I could find, I asked him if he knew what he had done wrong. He admitted to pushing Tabby. I discussed everything that was wrong with violence and why we must never use it as retaliation. I asked for confirmation that he understood what I was saying. I never wavered in the strength of my words or tone. I followed all the rules.

There was only one problem: Since the light is better in Logan's room, I will sometimes do my makeup in there. That morning, apparently, I had left my makeup case behind. He had helped himself to some blue eye shadow which he streaked across his cheek. A little purple lipstick was around his mouth and chin. Mascara that he actually succeeded in applying to one set of lashes lay in clumps and bled below his eye.

I was engaged in conversation with a miniature drag queen.

When Nate arrived home that evening, he looked tired and frazzled. He gave me one of his half smiles that tells me to give him some space so he can shake off the workday before he put on his dad hat. I, however, was tired of wearing my Mom hat and decided whatever had happened in his day could wait. I told him of the altercation between Logan and Tabby. He took one look at his son and asked, "So you forced him to wear makeup?"

I laughed.

Logan said, "Yes."

"We need to talk," Nate said.

"I agree." I said. "How about in Bermuda? I'll call Mary."

"I'm serious," he said. "What happened?"

I saw that he was getting agitated. I sent the kids to their rooms to play. Nate tried to sort out the details. I became increasingly infuriated as he pinched the bridge of his nose, which indicates what I am saying is giving him a headache. A cry came from Tabby's room. I rolled my eyes and went off to see what had happened. I stood in the doorway of Tabby's room undetected. Tabby was holding a doll at a tea party she had set up. She could not get the doll to stay upright in a sitting position. Every time she released it, the doll would fall to the side. Tabby balled her little fists and made a noise from her throat. Logan turned around from the puzzle he was working and asked Tabby what was wrong. He even put a hand on her shoulder. She turned her watering blues to Logan and pointed to the doll.

"Not working," she said and demonstrated by trying to sit the doll once more. Tears rolled down her cheeks.

"Let's try this!" Logan said, jumping up. He brought a book over and made a tent of it behind the doll. The doll gently reclined on it.

Tabby was thrilled. "Than ew, Logun," she said and began pouring the imaginary tea.

"You're welcome, Tabby."

They proceeded to play in harmony, Tabby at her tea party and Logan at his puzzle. I took a deep breath and returned to the living room. I sat down next to Nate and asked how his day had been. He said "Fine" curtly and leaned back in his chair. When he looked at me, I smiled, inviting him to elaborate. Slowly, he did. The more he talked, the more he relaxed. When he was done, we revisited the kid's altercation and aftermath. When I told it now, we both snickered, then laughed. I like laughing with Nate. He is a nice companion to be going through all of this with.

Especially if we go through it in Bermuda.

Chapter Fourteen

Swimming in Lake Me

The other day, Nate asked me if I wanted some "Me Time." I probably should have mentioned the overwhelming sense of the walls closing in on me long before he mentioned the twitch in my left eye whenever I looked at the children. But I took his suggestion. Me Time is short lived. I took a night to get my nails done—("a night" equates to 3.75 hours in Momhood time).

Once I returned, Nate felt owed. I don't mean sexually; that is what jewelry is for. I mean *he* wanted some Me Time. He checked out to surf the internet for six hours. However, it was 9:00 P.M., and the children were just finishing dinner. Pajamas, teeth brushing, stories, songs and the general battle to get them to stay in bed had not yet begun. I asked as to what, perchance, delayed the bedtime ritual? He didn't know. They were just messing around.

Why bother? I had to play catch up, and I was out 50 bucks for the nails that subsequently got smudged.

So I tried a slightly different approach. After the children were down, I poured my third glass of wine and told Nate, "The *funniest* things happen today. Right after lunch, Tabby decided instead of finishing her grape juice at the table, she would take it with her. Once on the couch, she decided to dump the juice out. No reason—just turned the cup over. But that wasn't the funny part. The funny part is, when I saw it, everything in my vision took on a red filter. That's right; I saw red—bright red—blood red, really. And then it all became kind of fuzzy, and I realized I was shaking . . . I know, weirdest thing, but I was shaking—my whole body.

So I went to the Mommyverse and asked others if this had ever happened to them and what they did about it. Some of the Mommyverse suggested I take a day off! How about that? You've gone white again. No, I don't mean I am going to actually leave the house and have you watch the kids. I mean I am just going to let you take point tomorrow. I will maybe take a bath, catch up on some reading—get a few things done. Of course, I will help out if you need it, but *you* will be the Main Parent tomorrow. What do you think?"

Here is how my day off went:

My bath is peppered with cries from the children who now HAVE to have a bath despite their protests and claims of tortures the night before. Nate comes in every five minutes, asking where something is, how is it going, do I want the children to come in? I begin to shave my legs when the children break in. They launch themselves into the bath with me. Nate realizes he has lost the children and comes to find them. When he sees them with me, regardless of the fact that they are still in pj's sitting in a full bathtub, he says, "Oh, good. You have them. I am going to run to work really quick to grab something. I'll be back in about twenty minutes."

Twenty minutes becomes a hundred twenty minutes, as per usual. I feed them and get Tabby to take a nap. I sit on my lawn chair and start reading. Nate, recently returned, gets me a soda. What a guy. He goes back in the house, presumably to get his own soda. Logan immediately needs something—anything. He needs to re-create *Starry Nights* in sidewalk chalk, and can I help him? He needs to learn arithmetic right now. He is interested in changing the brakes on the car—and so on. I realize Nate is missing. I go to find him only to discover he is asleep in our bed, where he stays for another hour. By the time he wakes up (with the requisite "Wow. I must have really needed that") it is time for dinner. Nate mentions how much he likes the way **I** cook steak.

The next day I call The Mothers. They laugh at me. They remind me how there never was such a thing as Me Time in their day. The only Me Time they were allowed was when they gave birth. I thank them again for birthing and raising me and Nate and plead some child emergency to get off the phone.

I call Gigi and Dawn because surely they must have similar experiences. Dawn is at lunch with her husband, her nanny Selma tells me. Gigi is thrilled I called because she has had the most amazing weekend with her family and tells me all about it. She asks what I wanted to say. I tell her that I should go and will call her tomorrow.

I sigh, and just then Nate walks in with a sad little arrangement of flowers he bought from the guy standing at a traffic light. He says we can order in tonight, and I put the flowers in water. He tells me he loves me, and I think maybe this really is a nice life.

Chapter Fifteen

Potty Training

Potty training is difficult for some and a piece of cake for others. Below I shall include all of the methods I have found to be effective and everything I know about potty training after having trained two children:

Chapter Sixteen

Exalt Every Action

The other day, Logan's room was a disaster. I stood in his doorway and told him we had to straighten up and get ready to go because it was time to go meet his little friend Greystoke at the park for our playdate. No response. I reminded him that he had pestered me all last week to call Greystoke's mom for this playdate and we must not be late. Logan dropped his toys and started walking out of his room.

"No, no, Logan. We must clean up our room before we leave."

He continued to walk into the kitchen and stuck his head in the fridge.

"Logan, you just had breakfast and snacks. I don't want you eating anything else. Get out of that refrigerator and come back into your room. Pleeeease."

He circled around to the living room and started watching TV.

"Logan Princeton Unicef! You come in this room right now, or I will tell Greystoke's mom that we cannot play today!" There is a possibility he knew I would not do this. I never have before.

When I had gone pink in the face, Logan meandered into his room and dropped a block into the toy chest. I clapped and proclaimed, "Good job! Atta boy! Such a good boy, Logan!"

I effused over his efforts, if you could actually call what he was doing effort. Any time any item was placed somewhere other than where it was originally, I jumped around and sang "Logan's a great kid" songs. After twenty minutes and four items back where they belong, he tottered off to pilfer a banana.

Well, he had tried, hadn't he? So I finished picking up his room and made his bed. On our way out, I asked him to throw away the peel of his banana. He deposited the peel into the trash can, and I got teary. Somebody's getting a treat from Toys&More for being such a good helper!

I reward anything these days. Once Tabby wet her pants but the urine did not actually reach the floor. I gave her three M&Ms. My friends are no different. Dawn bought the twins bikes because they went a whole week without making her cry. Gigi's son Schubert once saved a baby bird that had fallen from its nest, and Gigi donated a new ornithology exhibit to their local zoo in his honor.

We acknowledge *everything*. I keep confetti on hand in anticipation for the *First* we are about to experience—"Tabby used the TV remote control all by herself! Hurray!" (Nate, call the cable company and get a new remote, would you? This one doesn't seem to function anymore.) "Oh, boy. Logan went the whole day without dumping the dog food in the washing machine! Pizza time!"

I attended Logan's soccer game on Saturday. The game was for three to five-year-olds. No score was kept so that no one would be disappointed. There was a shindig after the game. We acknowledged either everyone winning or maybe nobody losing. I am not quite sure. We had hot dogs; burgers; cakes; and syrup-heavy, neon-colored drinks. During our celebration we recapped pivotal moments in the game that didn't really affect the outcome because we did not keep score.

Every "How to Raise a Kid" book tells you that positive reinforcement is the way to go. If you react to good behavior and not bad, the children will seek out that reaction, and you foster good behavior. The results of this were evident at a playdate I went to just last week. Tabby, Logan and I went to their friend Newru's house. Also, there was a pair of twins named Petunia and Gladiola. Our mothers might have scooped us up and thrown us outside with the door locked behind us. The other moms and I, however, attempted a friendly chat with our children present. As we dodged various projectiles whizzing across the room, we tried desperately to keep focus on what the other was saying.

Meanwhile, the children were hitting and scratching and pulling and pushing and anything else that elicited shrieks from their victims. In one conflict, Newru's mom said to her son, "Oh, Newru, we don't like to hit our friends, do we? Go give Petunia a kiss and say sorry."

"No?"

(To Petunia) "Newru is sorry, Petunia."

(To Newru) "Aren't you, Newru?"

Petunia's mom tried to dismiss Newru's actions as minor and probably deserved. Petunia's mom assured Newru's mom that Petunia bleeds easily and the trickle of blood coming from her mouth could be from anything.

Periodically a kid did something that was *not wrong*—not necessarily right but not wrong. This child was held up as an example for all the other children, "Look at Gladiola! She is sitting there tearing up that magazine and not bothering anyone!"

(To Gladiola's mom) "Oh, no, I wasn't going to read that one anyway." We launched into a regular cheer section. "All Praise Gladiola who didn't bother us in the last five minutes."

Since my children did not actually draw blood and only broke a few toys, I rewarded them by having pudding for dinner.

Not surprising, The Mothers don't exactly see eye to eye with me on this matter. They believe a *good* boy is one who does what you say the first time. They let me know that, when I held a job, my superiors did not huddle around my chair, lauding me for performing the tasks I was hired to do. They warn me that, when Tabby turns in her paper to her Berkeley professor as assigned, it might just come back with an A, not a marching band trumpeting its arrival. When adult Logan succeeds in *not* throwing his briefcase at the neighbor who waves hello, a messenger from above may not come down with a trunk of gold (or candy) for such actions.

But then, again, what do they know? Raising kids is different today.

Chapter Seventeen

Celebrate Good Times . . . and Every Other Event Too!

The other day I attended a pretty special celebration, a graduation. I have always been fond of graduations because I feel like they are a symbolic door opening to the future of the graduate. Will they be going to high school where their talent will be awakened? Are they leaving for college where a whole new world of intellectualism and enlightenment awaits them? Or perhaps they are entering the real world and the rest of their adult life is brimming with possibilities.

I like birthday parties, but it doesn't seem like the guest of honor has to do anything but survive to get one. Weddings are always lovely, but I find myself making bets with the other guests as to how many weddings the bride/groom will have. (If I like the person with whom I place the bet, I make plans to sit at their table at the next one). But graduations are both a sense of accomplishment and a chance to expand one's potential.

This graduation celebration I attended was no different. There were speeches by school dignitaries. Mothers were weeping over their children growing up. Graduates took the stage to commemorate what they had learned. Bouquets were everywhere—balloons and cards abounded. Relatives traveled far and wide to attend. The excitement in the room was palpable.

Logan's four-year-old friend Addison was graduating from the Fluffy Clouds class to the Big Rainbows class. She was in a cap and gown.

Her parents held a catered lunch in their backyard after the ceremony. It was themed "Influential Women in Music," given Addison's newfound love of the kazoo. At my table, some of the other moms compared this event to some of theirs. (For those of you who don't know, "comparing" in Mom talk means "lambasting.") It was a gently worded war to see who loved her child more. For Sunshine's first day of eighth grade, her mom made a colorful banner adorned with smiling suns (nice tie-in). On Pylon and Fleur de Lys' first day of third grade, their moms thought it would be cute to dress in their old cheerleading uniforms. They wrote cheers and chanted them out front of the elementary school as their children emerged. Aloysius' mom had a bouncy house on retainer, just in case.

That night I called Dawn. It was no use going to Gigi on this one. My self-esteem had bottomed out. I told her about Addison's graduation and my talk with the other moms. I asked what she did for parties.

"Oh, we blew out the doors for the twins' preschool graduation party."

"You did?"

"Yeah—the Circus Theme, remember?"

"The one with the animals and the professional clowns?"

"Yep, almost had a high wire act across the telephone poles, but the City pulled the permits at the last minute."

"For their *preschool* graduation. Why?"

"Honey, you forget. With my twins, this may be the only graduation I attend."

For Tabby's last birthday, I went to a park with some other families and relied on the playground to entertain the kids. Was I denying my children the inalienable right to celebration? To date, I had not celebrated anything aside from birthdays. How was I to know Logan's first tooth loss should have been heralded to the world? I am thinking of digging it out, reinserting it and doing the whole thing over.

A few months back I was waiting for Logan's class to get out for the day. I was standing next to Petunia and Gladiola's mom. To make conversation, I asked her for some birthday party ideas. She panicked.

"Oh! I am so bummed you brought that up—I am totally unprepared!"

"You? Really?" I asked, incredulous.

"Oh, Lord, yes. I have no idea what the theme is going to be. I mean, I have the cake ordered from *Celebrities Buy Our Cakes. Party Planners to the Stars* is contracted, but until they get the theme, how can they customize the gift bags? Of course, I have the bouncy house reserved."

"When is their birthday?"

She shudders, "August."

Then I shudder, "It's still January, right?"

"Yes," she said, wide eyed. I left her and went to the bank.

I opened "Celebrations" savings accounts for both my kids. I was covered for graduations: Tabby's Sweet Sixteen and Logan's Studly Eighteen (this may not be an actual right-of-passage, but I was taking no risks). The nice man at the bank set everything up and looked up at me with a smile of anticipation.

"How much for the Big One?"

"Big One? What Big One? Who Big One?" I asked.

"Your daughter's wedding?"

Do they make a bouncy house that big?

Chapter Eighteen

Open House

 I think the thing that scares me most these days is when the phone rings and the person on the other end of the receiver says, "Oh, I will just pop over for about five minutes." As I exclaim my excitement of an impromptu get-together, I look around my house in horror. Somehow, unbeknownst to me, a Toyland Megastore's delivery truck was rerouted and dumped its contents on my living room floor. No worries. I will merely shove the entirety of the living room into the kids' rooms and shut the door. Oops, the truck got in there too. Maybe I could put it into my room? I'll just say that I have unfolded laundry in there and giggle in embarrassment. Unfortunately, the laundry story is true, and the mound of clothes waiting to be put away on my bed is threatening to crush me.

 Perhaps this mess will fit in the kitchen cupboards? Oh, good, they are empty! Because the children have recently emptied their entire contents on to the kitchen floor. Nuts. I slip on the baking mix blanketing my floor. Right before I crack my head on the jam-smeared counter, I think:

 "Maybe we can have a nice chat in the backseat of the car?"

 A few questions come to mind. First, what the hell do I do all day if my house looks like this? Second, how can I peg this on the either Nate or The Mothers? And, last, what is acceptable house presentation when someone—especially a fellow mom—drops by?

 In my SWOC days and before I could afford an actual cleaning crew, I would scrub my tiles with a toothbrush on the eve of an impending visit. It didn't matter who was coming. I would don night vision goggles to get that last dust bunny in the corner. After I married, I maintained this level of precision in my visitor preparedness by simply no longer inviting so many people over. After I became a mother, I realized that my days of a sparkling house for visitors were numbered and that Nate would not agree to us being shut-ins. So I developed a new rule for visitors: I would do the massive clean for a person visiting for the first time—first impression and all. After that, my efforts would decrease with each subsequent visit.

This seemed to work for a while. I did have to reconsider my efforts when The Mothers pulled a fictile piece of what I can only guess was cheese off of the arm of my sofa. These days, a visitor is fairly lucky if I make a path for them through the toys and clothes that litter my floor. Baking mix on some part of their clothes is a given.

Unfortunately, mothers are women, and nobody has found a better bar by which to measure ourselves than our fellow women. So if Peggy Perfect is walking on gleaming floors at her house, you better make sure you are too. I always make the same disclaimer "Oh, please do come over—but be prepared. My house is a mess" and then I lock the children in the closet, tie the dog to a pole and use him as a push broom to get everything under furniture. I am a master at spot cleaning. I can zap any splotch adorning my floor into submission in no time flat. And if the spot-cleaning doesn't work? Throw a rug over it

And those times when I do put the effort? The times that I have broken out cleaning supplies and gloves and towels reserved for the act of cleaning? I scrub and scrape and vacuum and dust and do everything I ever saw The Mothers do in my youth to produce a house worthy of visitors. As soon as the visiting mom crosses the threshold, a swipe of what you hope to high heaven is chocolate pudding that has been streaked across a perfectly white wall stands out like the Vegas strip at night. In all the hours you disinfected every surface, how did this glaringly obvious sign of your inadequacies disguise itself?

So I gave up. Perky Playtime Music Tables serve as end tables. Giant Buddy Bears act as wingback chairs (with the right draping). I send people their drinks and appetizers in Tinker the Traveled Train cars. Kid Chaos is the new Shabby Chic. If people need a plate, I have old album covers that aren't being used. Coaster? Why? Having the house look like a carnival threw up in it reflects my life just fine. If I wanted to put on an air of sophistication, I would need to read something a smidge above the intellectual musings of OK! magazine anyway.

If Perfect Peggy's gleaming floors make you feel inferior, just start a rumor that her house has rats.

Chapter Nineteen

Guerilla Warfare

Here is an interesting conundrum: You have this amazing partner. You enjoy having sex with this amazing partner. The sex is amazing. The sex is fun. The sex produces children. The children are desired results of the sex. When the children producing ceases, the fun sex is still desired. The children, produced from the sex, do everything in their power to prevent the fun sex. Why? Do they not see how much happier Mom is after she and Dad have one of their "Talks" behind closed doors? Why?

Here are a few ways in which Nate and my sex life has changed since our children have come into being:

First, our language of love is less melodic and more utilitarian. Nate and I used to take each other's hands over a candle-lighted table and mouthed words of desire and love to each other. The other day I was wearing a T-shirt that was too tight. Nate pointed and said, "Hi, girls!" That's about it for foreplay these days. Instead of "I just had to wake you up because I could not take another minute without you in my arms" has become "Wait. Is it Wednesday already?"

Second is in time devoted to the act. Pre-kids, we would invest an entire night to being together. Now we slip it in between items on our to-do list. An odd phenomenon has occurred as a result: a Pavlovian response to the theme song of our children's favorite show "Sure You Can!" By some mystic coincidence Nate and I complete most of our morning tasks right around the time this show comes on. So with the kids perfectly occupied by the "Can Doers" for 30 minutes, we look at each other and sneak off for about seven minutes (let's not candy-coat it). I have never seen "Sure You Can!" but I would nominate it for a Peabody Award.

The third change is in execution. Instead of a slow passionate expression of our love, we hope to have sex with as little effort and time involved as possible. The other day, Logan came looking for us. We thought we had a moment, but we underestimated a toddler's desire to see "That Silly Mouse" for the 477th time. We were *engaged* in our room when we heard:

"Moooom?" and the soft padding of feet.

Silence followed. We thought we were clear to resume. Soon our bedroom door opened partially and then slowly shut. We convinced ourselves that would be our only interruption. A few minutes later, the door burst open, and Logan came scrambling up on our bed.

"MOM!" he said excitedly.

"What do you need, Logan?!" I asked securing my grandmother's quilt over any exposed flesh.

My son threw a catalogue next to me and pointed to a picture for a specially designed four-step ladder meant for elderly dogs.

"We need this for Scruffy." he said, determined.

"No, we don't," I countered.

"Yes we do," he pursued.

"Scruffy is not an old dog, and he can get on the bed just fine—see." I said pointing at the aforementioned Scruffy who was now sitting at the foot of the bed licking Nate's calf.

"No, he needs it."

"Logan, we do not need to get that for Scruffy. Maybe when he is an old man dog and he cannot bounce up on the bed, but right now he is fine."

"But Mooommmmm!"

Nate jumped in. "Fine, Logan. We will get it—now go check on your sister."

Logan left victorious. Scruffy came up and dropped his saliva-laden chew toy next to my ear. I tried to ignore him; so he nosed the disgusting piece of rope closer to me, wetting my cheek. Tabitha came into the room and began spinning down the side of the bed until she fell over, taking my alarm clock with her. I turned to Nate and said, "I think we are done here."

He looked at the fallen Tabitha and Scruffy who had gotten the rope wedged between the headboard and the mattress and was growling furiously.

"We'll just say you owe me," he said, robing himself.

"Fine," I said. "And we will say the same for you." To punctuate my point, I pressed Logan's catalog, now turned to the jewelry section, into his chest.

He laughed and grabbed Tabby's stuffed cat and began to playfully chase her with it. Her squeals almost made up for my lost morning.

Scruffy never did get his ladder. I *did* get my jewelry.

Chapter Twenty

Feeling Sexy

Sometimes I have good mornings. Maybe I have stayed on my diet a bit more than usual. Maybe my hair hit a high point—something that makes me feel a little sexier than the day before. On these days, I like to act on this feeling and milk it for all it is worth. So I do what I did in my SWOC days, I put on those jeans that I usually cannot wear (without others exclaiming "Oh, dear.") I opt for a top that shows a little more skin (SWOC days—this meant a little cleavage. Mom days—this mean my collarbone finally gets some sunlight.) I fluff the hair and even find the will to slap a little gloss on the pucker. On these days, I feel good. In my SWOC days, I carried this feeling until bedtime. In Mom days, it lasts until breakfast.

I sashay out of the bedroom in my come-hither jeans and maybe a shoe with a small heel. Logan has decided to make pancakes but never got past the baking mix. He, Tabby, the dog, the counter and the bench in the foyer are dusted in white powder mix (seriously, what is their obsession with the damn baking mix?!?) With the tablespoon of mix that actually landed in the bowl, he added seven cups of water and is vigorously whirling it with a spatula. A few random drops hit my hair, to be discovered later.

At the mall, I walk to the car, and a trio of dapper young businessmen gives me a shy smile as I pass. I feel quite sassy. I don't see the chocolate handprint on my left breast until I start the ignition. At lunch, I notice the waiter glancing at my mouth. I use many words that cause my lips to purse and bat my eyes. Finally he asks me if I am bleeding. I don't think so. He points to my chin. Why, yes, it appears I am bleeding. I can only guess it is some pimple that got scratched inadvertently. He gives me extra whipped cream on my dessert. I take his pity. The rest of my day goes along these lines.

I don't know what happens. Nate walks in after nine hours of work, which includes three grueling meetings and LA traffic both ways and looks sexily disheveled. I make it out of the shower and people start asking if I feel all right. I was never a beauty queen. I held my place as wingman to all my pretty friends, but at least I was clean.

The Mothers used to set their hair with those giant rollers and tie a scarf around it and ran errands. They looked cool. When they removed their rollers, their gleaming hair tumbled across their shoulders. They slipped on one of those floor-length dresses moms in the 70s wore and kohled their eyes. By the time they opened the door to our returning dads' with a martini in hand, they looked like they stepped out of a Halston ad.

If I put rollers in my hair, at some point I am forced under the couch to retrieve an errant ball or behind a chest of drawers to pick up a rotting banana. When I come back up, my rollers have acted as a magnet for cobwebs and dust. The dog runs from me in horror. Interjecting myself between two brawling children will result in various blows and hair-pulling—mine. By the time I go to get the rollers out, they are so snaggled with hair I have to cut them out or wear them until my hair decides to fall out on its own.

I can't walk around with a coffee cup without fear of someone throwing change in it.

So I have cut off our cable and all magazine subscriptions that might show a female form. I come home, slip into some comfortable pajamas, peel the candy off my cheek and flop down on the couch. Nate comes in and stands there just staring at me. When I meet his eyes, he smiles.

"What?" I ask.

"The way the light is hitting you right now. You look amazing."

I wave him off.

He sits next to me on the couch and kisses me gently. "Honestly, you just keep getting more beautiful with age. Every woman you know must envy you."

I lay my head into his chest. Kids must be a good look for me.

Chapter Twenty-One

MINE!

Among the various religious, political and social topics Nate and I discussed prior to marriage, we agreed that one of us would stay home to raise the children. *We* decided this. It was not an ultimatum or a concession. Since Nate made a larger salary than I, we settled on me being the SAHP.

I had earned some form of salary since my early teens. Sometimes it was a ridiculously minimal salary, and sometime I spent it on shoes when I should have paid bills, but I earned my own money for most of my life. So it was no little thing for me to say, "Sure. I'll stay at home while you continue to work." But I was excited by the possibilities.

When I quit working, Nate thought, since I had a little more time on my hands, I could take over a few other things—things that really went under the umbrella "running the house" anyway. I added to my list of *To Dos* laundry, ironing, meals, housekeeping, shopping (food, clothing, household, etc), car maintenance, yard maintenance, house maintenance, total financial output, childcare, taxi service and medical caregiver. At first, this was quite heady. I had complete control over everything. I thought I was Superwoman.

But I am not Superwoman, and things soon seemed to unravel. The kids are alive, if not necessarily enjoyable. The house is standing, even if it was on pillars of dirty laundry and yesterday's breakfast dishes. About the time my inadequacies as a housewife started to peek through, Nate slipped in a few jokes about taking himself to work so that I might live in the manner in which I was accustomed (titter) or a casual mention of how nice it is not to have to get out of sleepwear before lunch, if at all (tee-hee) or how fun it must be to get to do crafts and make cupcakes instead of going to meetings (ha-ha). And I took these in the good fun they were intended. But one little phrase crept into Nate's vocabulary that did not go unnoticed:

"My money."

More jokes popped up like "Honey, may I have my money to go buy a new CD?" Then points were made, all with a laugh, "You bought me my Father's Day gift with my money—so actually I bought it." And other times, there was no joke, "What do you mean I shouldn't have bought a new computer without consulting you—it's my money."

I tried to assure myself that I did contribute to the family in a most valuable way. The Mommyverse sent me links for calculators that tabulated how much salary a mom would earn if she was in the corporate world. I relished in the fact that my salary, according to these calculators, would surpass Nate's.

But my satisfaction was short lived because I did not earn any salary and what I do does not have a dollar value. So when I buy a little blouse on sale for 30 percent off, I feel guilt. And when I get the kids some new pajamas, I contemplate if they actually need them or if they would enable me to put laundry off for one more day. Despite everything, the dollar wins. And despite my knowing everything to the contrary, I bow to the fact that I am not a wage earner.

This fight is not a new one. Women have had this battle for ages. The only time in conscious memory The Mothers jumped in and defended *me* was after Nate made a "my money" joke in front of them. They descended on him like locusts.

The point is it is not funny. When I have finished pretending I know how to raise children and try to get back in the workforce, I will have a terrible uphill climb. My resume is shot because I have a gap in my experience. I know this because, when I was hiring, I tossed out SAHM's resumes for this reason. I have committed career suicide.

Dawn and Gigi cannot relate on this one. Dawn has the money in her family. Their lavish lifestyle and the arsenal of help they employ come from her trust fund. Gigi's husband makes a very nice living, and things are never tight for them. Even if they were, Gigi is too good at what she does to bring up money.

I turn to the only person I can—Nate. I remind him of our decision and how we chose for one of us to stay home. I mention how insecure the money comments make me. He apologizes and tells me he meant nothing by them—and then makes them again after he's forgotten our discussion. I lick my wounds and tell myself they are just jokes and Nate would never actually consider me unequal. As I carry my wounded ego around in a dishtowel, I happen upon Nate on the phone. He does not know I am there. Before I return to the kitchen,

I overhear him say, "I can't relate to you there, buddy. My wife is the greatest. She runs this entire house. She has to be the best mother in the world. I don't know what we would do without her."

So I close the door quietly with a tear in my eye and love filling my heart and feel really bad about putting the diuretic in his steak sauce.

Chapter Twenty-Two

Let's Talk About It

I love to talk. I would do it all the time if I could. So you can imagine what it does to a talker when you reduce the collective intellect of the audience to a litter of puppies. Instead of insightful and thought-provoking dialogues on the current administration's economic policies, I debate the merits of eating two cookies after lunch versus the one given. I try to decipher exactly why the bath mat offends Tabby so much. I laud picture after picture of scattered pen strokes which are supposed to be a monkey/princess/stop sign. When I ask the artist what their motivation was, the response is generally "Because." I discuss the pros and cons of dancing on the coffee table and how you could still get hurt, even if you have done it before.

I watch children programs and try to engage my children in dialogue as to why what the protagonist did that day was right or wrong. But they don't care, and neither do I. And don't get me started on the literature I discuss now. I have bid the damn Moon Good Night. Now leave it!

The complex and modified sentences I once uttered are reduced to "Do you need to make a potty?" My last debate closer was "Because Mom likes those shoes and the orange juice does not belong in them."

The other day, Logan came out of his room and was desperately trying to explain something to me. I was so excited for the discourse we were about to have.

"I . . . I . . . I . . . the truck is has green and POW . . . but can't . . . I build a tower for the dragon ship and . . . hmm . . . ." He turned and ran back in his room.

I waited.

I called to him in his room. "What was that now?" I asked

"Nothing!" he said defensively.

"No, you are not in trouble. What were you trying to tell me?" I ask gently, albeit eagerly.

"Nothing! I'm okay, Mom."

"No, Logan . . . I want to know . . ." but I was cut short as Tabby walked in with her head and one arm through the leg of her shorts and wearing a cereal box as a hat. "Hi Mom!" she said enthusiastically.

I try to observe the rules in the "How to Raise a Kid" books. I set them down for discussions on their behavior.

"Why did you hit Tabby, Logan?"

"Why? Because I hit her."

"No, I know what you did. Why did you do it?"

"Why? Because I pulled her hair."

"No, I know that . . . wait—what? I thought you hit her?"

"No, I pulled her."

"You pulled her? You mean you pushed her?"

"Yes."

"Why?"

"Because the ground."

"I know where. Why?!?"

"Because . . ."

"Oh, never mind. Just don't do it again."

I love when people call me. A telemarketer who only wants me to protect my credit card needs to be prepared to discuss what happened to the Republican Party I registered for at 18. Clean my carpets? First, give me information on that new star they discovered. Do I know where my tax dollars are going? No. Do you know why leggings have made a comeback? Donation? Absolutely—if you can tell me if this celebrity is really sleeping with that celebrity and why that person is an actual celebrity to begin with.

I used to hold these discussions with myself, but my children are at an age that they wonder why Mom is yelling at the coffee filter. I don't mind confusing my kids, but soon they might report my behavior to The Mothers, which could be admissible in court.

Of course, the one who gets unloaded on the most is Nate. After a long day of people throwing problems at him to solve or petty arguments he is asked to take a side on, he comes home to the children at their normal volume and a wife who is chewing on the corner of a newspaper. Nate and I are alike in many important ways, but we don't hold all the same interests. My maudlin fascination with all things celebrity eludes him. What sports teams have a shot at some title is of no consequence to me. When Nate walks in the door, I commence talking about whatever I want to talk about. Nate tries to field my ramblings, the kids' demands for attention and his own desperate need of a glass of wine.

At some point he puts up his hand and says, "Honey, I need a minute."

I get my feelings hurt because I feel unimportant and think whatever I am nattering on about is really interesting. I say okay with my best hurt voice and sulk off to the kitchen to finish dinner. After dinner, Nate tries to resuscitate the conversation. But I pout, and say that I don't feel like talking anymore, which is a lie because that is all I want to do. He tells me about his day to fill the void. I interrupt him and ask why he thinks his day is more important than mine. He says he *tried* to get me to tell him the rest of my story but I wouldn't. I decide to forgive him and start in again on everything going on in my mind. Nate smiles and nods. His eyes take on an opacity that I see from time to time when I talk. As Nate starts slumping down in his chair, I think how lovely it is that we can communicate like this.

Chapter Twenty-Three

Mimosa Mondays

The First Day of School. The golden ring for every mother is the time she gets to be alone. This is my year. Logan is going to kindergarten. On the first day of school, for three solid hours, I will be alone in my beautifully clean home with no noise, no demands and only *my* agenda to follow.

When the day is finally upon us, I wake in a dynamite mood. I make breakfast. I assemble nutritious lunches for all (including Nate—drawing a picture on his lunch bag for fun.) I sing the kids awake (Okay. This is not so much a treat for them as my singing voice is akin to a nail being pulled across the hood of a car.) I bring Nate his coffee in bed. Everyone is happy and eager to start their day—no one more ready than me. Three hours to myself. I am delirious.

I pile the kids in the car. Nate suggests that maybe he should stick around so we could have some Alone Time. "No, no. We don't need any of that nonsense," I think—unfortunately out loud. Quickly covering my tracks, I add, "Get to work so you can hurry home to me tonight!" I may regret that later.

First, I drop off Logan. I have a little trouble reading the Who Goes Where charts in the front of the school. I try six classrooms before I find a teacher who would take him. Checking my watch, I am only a few minutes behind my schedule. Still plenty of alone time left.

Tabby and I sing all the way to her new classroom. Our singing is cut short when Tabby bursts into tears. She wants her former classroom. I tell her this is a BIG GIRL classroom and Mom really needs to get home to her book, cup of coffee and silence. With my precious minutes ticking away, I point Tabby to the tissues and run out as she reaches for one.

Supermom Breaks A Nail

I am humming to myself when the director of the preschool stops me. Apparently I owe more for Tabby's monthly tuition. She is going her five days a week now, (yay!) and the rates increased some. I ask what I owe—anything to get out of here. I write the check. I will figure a way to cover it later when I am all by myself.

I am whistling weakly when I walk in to my house. It is not as clean as I had envisioned. But it *is* quiet and currently all mine. I sit on the sofa with my coffee and my book. I make a quick call to Nate. I need to tell him we have no more money so he shouldn't count on eating for a little while. There is laughter in the background when he answers. Nate is having trouble collecting himself. Turns out, my drawing on the lunch bag was not as recognizable as I had thought. Nate pinned it to the bulletin board and was holding a contest to see who could guess what the picture was. It was supposed to be Nate returning to the loving arms of his family after work. The closest anyone had gotten was a bear attacking a minimart. He offers up some other guesses. I tell him I don't have time for this and get back to my solitude.

I open my book. I keep eyeing the pair of shoes that need to be put away. As I go to pick them up, I knock over a stack of newspapers. I decide to run them out to the recycling can. It's when I am scrubbing my sink I remember my book and my now tepid coffee. As I put the orange juice away, I spy a half full bottle of champagne from the night before. Hmmm. I make myself a mimosa. The phone rings.

"Hi." Dawn says in the lowest, saddest way possible.

"What's up?" I ask.

Dawn had a bad weekend. She goes on to tell me about it. "What are you doing?"

"I am sitting here with a mimosa."

"A mimosa?" she asks.

"Sure. It's the first day of school."

"So it is. Let's see. Champagne, check. Juice? Check. OK, where was I?"

Dawn is a few minutes into a good rant when a beep comes through on her line. "It's the Shrimp. What's she doing? Hang on. I'll conference her in." She does so. "Hey, Gigi. It's both of us."

"Hi, girls." Another low voice. "My mother is coming tonight. I wasn't expecting her."

"Oh, honey. We're drinking mimosas—can you join us?" Dawn asks.

"Uhm, yes, I think I can. Here we are. Oh! And mango juice. Perfect"

"Perfect," we say.

We go a few rounds of *How My Life Sucks*. We pour some more drinks. Soon *How My Life Sucks* becomes *It Could Be Worse*. Another round. We start solving our problems, which makes us giggle. Another round. We start solving the world's problems, which makes us chortle. Another round. We cease trying to solve anything and simply laugh.

Dawn gets another beep. "Hang on." Dawn says. She clicks over.

Gigi and I talk about laundry.

Dawn clicks back. She is cackling. "My kids are already in the principal's office." Dawn says, barking out in laughter. "Day 1!"

We all fall on our respective couches howling. Dawn needs to go so we sign off. As soon as we do, my phone rings.

"Whatd'ya firgit?" I slur into the phone.

"Okay. We think we have it." Nate says. "Is the picture you drew Big Foot applying for a job at Hooters?"

"Yes. Now, git yer butt home. No use wasting an empty house."

Chapter Twenty-Four

I'll Climb Any Mountain

I am not a crafty person. My friends tell me that making things together makes up a large part of *family time*, that is, until the children learn how to play board games and the craft closet is converted into a hideaway bar. As soon as I had a child, my inbox was cluttered with links to fun crafts for kids and how to make your baby's time meaningful. I was not aware a baby's time had to be meaningful. I thought it just had to survive. But apparently a baby needs to survive AND do crafts.

I never lost my joy of holidays; so this seemed as good a place as any to start with the crafts. Unfortunately, I started when Logan was 10 months old, and the most he got out of making his own Christmas stocking was to gnaw on some felt and somehow glue the foot of his all-in-one suit to the tablecloth.

Although clearly not cut out for this kind of thing, I diligently assembled my Santa/turkey/Menorah/Easter basket/Valentine's Day Card/shamrock/I Have A Dream Journal alongside my children. I offered bits of history about the holiday we were celebrating for cultural enrichment. I spend a great deal of time on material acquisition, craft research, baking and craft area preparation. The children would come in, spot the glitter tube, dump its contents on a pool of glue they had poured and ask to watch TV. I would spend the next week scraping stickers off my floor.

I bought kits once, thinking maybe we would all enjoy it more if it was easier on me. But I made the mistake of calling Gigi to tell her about my craft day.

"Oh, a kit! You are so smart," she began. "I think I just lost a year of my life stressing over finding muslin for the Three Wise Men's cloaks."

I knew I should not have asked, if I valued my own self-worth, but I did anyway. "Muslin?"

"Yes. It is often depicted that they wore velvet and silk and other warm, luxurious fabrics. In fact, the Bethlehem census took place in the summer. And they were traveling. They were *wise* men after all; they would not have been bogged down with cumbersome robes."

"Are Sonnet and Schubert in a Christmas pageant?"

"No. Why?"

Halloween seems to bring out the crafter in most people as well. When we were young, The Mothers made our costumes from scratch and often had to change the costume when we changed our mind as to what we wanted to be. Our costumes were both historically accurate and terribly complex. I cut a picture out of a magazine and tape it to my kid's shirt.

For once, Dawn cannot make me feel better. She is the craft queen. She bedecked our college dorm with rugs made out of our discarded tee-shirts. Craft time is the one time Selma is sent to the store and Dawn dazzles her twins with her ingenuity. What that woman can fashion from a pipe cleaner, a paper napkin and an address label is amazing.

But I do my best and I never gave up. Until . . .

The Wing Incident.

I found some little Ladybug wings for Tabby in a catalogue. Since ladybugs were her insect-du-jour at that time, I ordered them. When they arrived, Tabby put them on and ran around singing "Ladybug!" as Logan ran behind her flapping the wings. Soon discord occurred. Tabby did not want her wings flapped and would tersely admonish Logan for each infraction. I told Logan that they were, in fact, Tabby's wings and he needed to abide by her wishes.

Soon the pleas came. Logan *desperately* needed some ladybug wings. He *had* to have them. Could I *puh-leeeeze* make them for him. Somehow I came to the conclusion that, yes, yes, I think I can make wings.

I spent the next 40 minutes disassembling wire hangers and re-forming them into beautiful little wings. I diligently taped the exposed edges with electrical tape so no precious skin got pierced. Logan selected tissue paper for me to fold around wires. I made armbands from coordinating ribbon. I even thought to tie the ribbon in knots at the point of entry so the wings would not flap about willy-nilly. My wings were gorgeous. Insects outside gazed in with avarice at my wings. My wings were not a craft; they were art.

I excitedly turned to Logan and showed him his beautiful butterfly wings. He shot out of his chair with a chirp, grabbed his wings and put them on. We ran to the full length mirror, and his smile stretched from ear to ear. As soon as they were in place, Logan threw his elbows back to flap his wings. After one flap of his wings, he removed the arm straps and allowed them to drop carelessly to the floor. He proceeded to walk out the door.

"Wait!" I screeched as he started for the door. "Why did you throw your wings down?"

"I didn't fly," Logan said in a voice that sounded like "*Duh.*"

Chapter Twenty-Five

No Small Sacrifice

I have loved Barbies my whole life. When I was a little girl, I had a two-by four-foot suitcase that held two Barbies, and the rest was clothes. The men in my life should have known they were never getting any part of the closet space. I put the Barbies away, reluctantly, at whatever age you were supposed to do that.

Tabitha was recently given her first Barbie. She is enamored of it. So I got it in my craw to look for those Barbies from my youth. I went into our attic in the garage and snooped around—no pink and white trunk. But I did find my *other* Barbies—the designer ones I got when I was older. These beautiful dolls with exquisite clothing were once displayed as art on shelves (in my SWOC days, when nobody could argue with me). Since Nate was reticent to having crowds of Barbies adorn our bedroom, I had squirreled them away in a comfortable temperature-resistant box until the day that I had a daughter who would appreciate them. Spotting them, I decided to bring them down for Tabby. Truthfully, I wanted to see them. They are beautiful, and I wanted to remind myself just how beautiful. Giving them to Tabby would allow me to see them every day and not feel bad about my unwavering love of those little plastic goddesses.

Tabby was astounded by the bounty of princesses that befell her. We carefully took them out one by one and reassembled shoes, stands and accessories. There they were—my girls. They were just as gorgeous as I remembered them. After the awe died down, Tabby asked me to play Barbies with her. This is why I had brought them out, wasn't it? But Dawn called; so I told Tabby to give me a minute, I would play as soon as I was off the phone. After I ended my call, I returned to the office to play Barbies.

And this is where the problem started.

The first sign of trouble was Tabby had rearranged the shoes. She had green shoes with a pink dress and navy shoes with a predominantly black dress. I laughed this off and promptly went about putting the correct shoes with the correct dress. Of course those little buggers popped off as soon as I got them on, which is why I got a little aggravated when Tabby started to switch them again. I halted all shoe-changing. This is when I noticed the stands. Some stands have the name clearly marked on them. Parisian Barbie does not go on the Beatrix Potter stand—I don't care if they both belong to the European Union. As I carefully explained the names on the stands and the Barbie they went with them, I saw Tabby trying to shove Ralph Lauren Barbie's arm into her camel overcoat.

"Tabby," I said in as even a tone as I could. "That overcoat just drapes over her shoulders. We do not put her arm in it."

"But it's a coat—it goes on," she says, shoving poor RL Barbie's arm further in the coat, wrinkling her double breasted navy blazer in the process. I grabbed RL Barbie and straightened the whole mess out. At this point, Tabby started fidgeting with Bob Mackie Barbie. She may be three; but, for Christ's sake—it's Bob Mackie.

"No, Tabby, the cape stays on."

"I don't like the hat."

"It's not a hat; it's the top of the cape. Stop trying to take it off. You will ruin it."

"I don't like it."

"IT'S BOB MACKIE!"

I distracted her with the hair brushes. Every little girl loves to brush Barbie's hair. She picked up a bright pink brush. Then she reached for Millennium Barbie. Millennium Barbie has a beautiful three-rolled, top-of-the-head bun with one perfectly coiled tendril falling to the side of her face. A brush would destroy it. I threw Birthday Barbie in Tabby's line of vision to distract her and sequestered Millennium Barbie to a safe spot. Then Tabby pointed and said, "Who's that princess?"

I love my daughter but I will be damned if she is getting her mitts on my Breakfast at Tiffany's Audrey Hepburn Barbie when she has shown no regard for maintaining these ladies' appearance. No discussion, I grabbed the doll and put her on my desk.

At this point Tabby took all the stands off and laid the Barbies on the carpet. "The princesses are sleeping," she said.

I could handle this. They were on the floor, yes, but no one was touching their hair. Our dog, Scruffy, decided it was time to give me a tongue bath. To get to me, he walked right across the Barbies in their repose.

"SCRUFFY!" I said, pointing at the beautiful little figures. Instead of recognizing the international sign for "Get Off My Damn Barbies, Mutt," he thought I wanted him to lick the Barbies instead. The more frantic my gestures became, the more confused Scruffy became.

This indicated to the cat, Fluffy, that it was time to play. So Tabby is trying to force Venetian Barbie's beautiful Carnivale mask into Christmas Cookie Barbie's hand; Scruffy is trampling these poor peaceful beauties; and Fluffy is tangled up in ball of synthetic hair and mesh overskirts. Logan came in asking for something as I was trying to control the carnage. I told him "Just a minute!" through gritted teeth. He stepped back right on to poor Cinderella Barbie's face.

"That's it! Playtime is over. Let's watch TV!" I bellowed.

And now I sit here, in my little office in which NO ONE is allowed, with my beautiful girls surrounding me. I gently tell them they may never see the light of day again.

Chapter Twenty-Six

Language Barriers

It is a common opinion that one should watch his or her mouth around children. Pretty much anything that pours forth from *your* mouth will spill out of *theirs* at any given moment —especially if that moment happens to be as you are trying to convince a headmaster of a prestigious private school that your little darling is the best choice to fill the one coveted opening left.

When I was pregnant with Logan, Nate and I agreed we had to curb our language. I am sure many parents will tell you this was not a problem because they don't really use bad language to begin with. Not us. People wonder if we know words with more than four letters in them. I can keep it together in the grocery store—until my favorite kind of cereal goes up 13 cents a box. Cell phones only increase the problem. I forget the world around me can actually hear me on a cell phone.

So I got pregnant, and we decided we needed to cut out the swearing. And we did... for about three days. All of a sudden, those nasty words started inching their way back into our vocabulary. We decided that maybe we should not go cold turkey. We tried to slowly eliminate the more colorful words from our repertoire until we run them all out. Every time we slipped, we reminded ourselves that we just needed to clean up our language by the time the baby is born.

In the meantime we cranked up the *Wolfgang Amino Mozart Pre Birth Selections* on my stomach and told each other what we really thought of our employers. Then the kid arrived. Our language dipped. Once again we rationalized. How much would the drooling grub retain anyway? We just needed to stop cursing by the time the kid was crawling. We were doing well, but then the crawling led to grabbing which led to pulling which led to things falling and breaking. That led to me proclaiming my dissatisfaction with said events. And I did not quote Shakespeare.

There was always rationale. Always some theory as to why our children will have selective deafness that will keep them from hearing profanity. And then our son started to speak. And by "speak," I mean parrot. I do believe the first thing he said to The Mothers was "Damn it!" Yet another vote for me for Mother of the Year.

But kids do know what you should and should not say. Dawn has an Uncle Duke, who works at the docks. Uncle Duke is about as stereotypical a dockworker as you can get. On a good day, he will only refer to you as a "panty-waist, son of a bitch." On bad days he will heighten his use of expletives and name-calling to an art form. But he is a cream puff around our kids. As a treat, we take them to see Uncle Duke at work.

One visit, he took the twins, Logan and Tabby around to see all the boats and equipment used in his trade. When they were almost done, a fork lift operator was unloading boxes. He turned the lift too quickly and knocked down a couple of cases of toilet paper. The rolls got loose and TP'd the dock. Uncle Duke, his supervisor, unleashed a torrent of words so filthy Quentin Tarantino would have blushed. He used every curse in the book and then started just making new ones up. The other workers circled around. Some were jotting down notes. After his diatribe of filth finished, Twin 2 walked up to him with his finger out ready to tsk.

In a very commanding voice for a four-year-old, Twin 2 wagged his finger at Uncle Duke and proclaimed, loudly, "UNCLE DUKE! You said a bad word!"

All eyes turned to Twin 2 in anticipation. Which word would he cite? There were so many to choose from.

Twin 2 planted both hands firmly on his hips and said, "You said 'stupid.'"

And it was true. Somewhere in the river of profanity, Uncle Duke had, in fact, said "stupid." To this day, whenever Uncle Duke says stupid, his co-workers make him put a quarter in a jar. Next month they are going on a cruise with their collection.

Chapter Twenty-Seven

General Admission

Last year I helped my girlfriend throw an engagement party for our friend. It was an elegant affair, for a backyard cocktail party. We even had *real* flowers. She has a child Tabby's age. We got my sitter, Mary, to watch all three at my house and waited expectantly in her backyard for all the stimulating conversation we were about to experience. As we stood there in our heels and big girl dresses and our husbands hovered by the appetizers, drinking martinis, the guests started to arrive. Imagine our surprise when the very first guests who entered came up to our knees.

My girlfriend and I looked in horror as the party area filled with children, not all of whom we even liked. In total, four couples brought their children to our cocktail attire-requested party. So regardless of paying $35 an hour for our own children to be watched, we spent the whole night chasing after kids, asking them not to touch all the food and to watch out as you may knock over one of the highboy tables . . . "Oh, dear, there goes the rhododendron."

When I took to the Mommyverse to ask if anyone else had had this experience, the response was not favorable . . . towards me. They said, if I did not want children, I should have clearly stated this on the invitation. Besides, what was the harm? Why could I not have just gotten one extra little table and put some fun foods on it for the kids? Had I just popped in a video, I would have been fine, they said.

Earlier this year, my cousin and her husband threw themselves a black tie anniversary party. Her sister asked what her daughter should wear to the party. The hostess cousin replied, "I assume whatever her sitter puts her in. Children are not invited to the party." Things, I am told, got ugly from there. I attended the party. It was lovely. I know it cost a fortune. There were half a dozen empty seats of parents who did not know until the last minute they could not bring their children—and one child in the corner, watching a video on an iPhone.

Being new to Momhood, I missed the day when the switch over from *Children are not invited unless specified* to *Children will always be included* happened. I labor for hours over the wording of a dinner invitation to insinuate that this is an adults-only evening without its sounding like I will provide strippers and a fishbowl. I have no problem with somebody asking me if kids are invited as long as they accept that no is a viable option. Occasionally I will respond to a child inquest with "No, this one is a night off for the parents! My own kids will be with their grandparents."

But then the invitee launches into a diatribe about how *they* don't really do things without their kids and *they* think their children are entertainment enough and don't need to exclude them to have fun. I assume that I am in the wrong and quickly retract the no-kids ban. I hang up and go hug my kids, apologizing once again for their great misfortune of having such a soulless mother. I spend the rest of the day thinking how to subtly let Nate know our wine and cheese evening is now a wieners and beans potluck.

So if we tell the Mommyverse that we need to get away from our little ones, where are we supposed to go if they are welcome everywhere? What about the amazing conversation we lament being absent from our lives? How in depth can you get on a topic when you have to interrupt with "Mom's talking to a grown-up now. Please get out of the flower pot." Heated political debates should not be paused to ask "Where did your pants go?"

I am not asking for the liberty to do keg stands, just the chance to not jump up and shove a wad of tissue in my conversation partners' face when they sneeze.

The flipside, of course, is actually going out. Nate had just been promoted to Super Cool, Extremely Important, Very Influential Employee at his work. By his rising to this august position, we received an invitation to a mixer for all the executives at his level or higher. This meant an evening of rubbing elbows with sophisticated people while sipping cocktails. I was so excited it caused me to hiccup.

Gigi, Dawn and I were on the phone every day trying to decide on an outfit. Since the first thing we decided was that my chosen outfit should have no food, spit, paint or drink stain on it, this eliminated three quarters of my wardrobe. I photographed myself on my cell phone, sent it to them and awaited their comments. One time I got a bit hasty in the contacts section and sent the photo to The Mothers by accident. They called me and asked for an explanation.

I explained, and they said to be more careful, that these risqué photos could be sent out to the whole world in a matter of minutes. I looked at the photo I had mistakenly sent. I am not sure slacks and a sweater set constitutes risqué these days. I guess it was the suede oxfords that pushed it over.

The day of the event came. I left myself a few hours to dress. Since Nate was not there, I asked my sitter to critique every detail. She smiled quizzically and said "Oh, yes, lovely. Very chic. Belt? Yes, that is a belt . . . oh, do I like it? Yes. But not necessarily with that top. I hope I am not stepping over the line. Perhaps I should just see to the children's dinner."

I was sitting perfectly still in my grown-up party outfit when Nate arrived. I had invested two hours into my appearance, and I looked acceptable at best. Nate raced in, spent four minutes assembling and looked stunning.

We blew kisses to the kids and off we went. I nervously tried out my topics of conversation in the car. "How about that stock market?" I said casually. "This is one humdinger of an election, don't you think?" I said with a whistle. "Boy, cancer research—could they use some more cash or what?"

"What are you doing?" Nate asked.

"Making small talk." I said.

He grabbed my note cards and threw them out the window. He was right; I should just ride his coattails.

The women in attendance looked exactly as they should. No matter how casual or formal, they were perfectly pulled together and wonderful looking. I could not stop adjusting my hair. I grabbed the first drink that came by. I did not know the man who had been holding the drink was not a waiter. The drink belonged to the Executive Director of Many Important Things. I spit the sip in my mouth back into the glass and offered his drink back to him. He politely declined.

Nate stepped in. A few moments later, he mingled us in and out of small collections of various people, each seemingly more important to the company than the next. I liked his tactic—keep us moving. Don't let me sit too long, or I might detonate like an unpinned grenade. As the evening wore on, my confidence came back to me. I did, after all, hold a college degree. I had traveled the world in my SWOC life. I taught myself to cook, regardless of what The Mothers say. I could certainly hold my own in this crowd.

At this point I had had several glasses of wine and very little food. Nate, recognizing the signs of Tipsy Wife, maneuvered us to a spot on the couch. A gentleman came by with a tray of little, artful pieces of food. I reached up to grab one and stopped myself. Since the guy I had stolen the drink from was sitting within earshot, I thought I would poke a little fun at myself, let people know I did not take myself too seriously. I looked up at the waiter and said "Are you really a waiter, or am I going to grab *your* stuff and put it in my mouth too?"

In my mind, this sounded breezy. The poor waiter's eyes grew very large and said "I . . . its tuna mousse in Filo cups."

A gentle woman to my left took pity on me and engaged me in conversation. I spent the rest of the evening speaking to her and the wife of Nate's boss. They were lovely ladies, and I really enjoyed our conversation—at least until Nate mentioned on the way home that I had spent probably a little too long talking about what I think takes smells off my hands best.

And when the head of the company sneezed within an arm's reach, I reached out and put a tissue under his nose.

Chapter Twenty-Eight

Mother Knows Best

I have spent thousands on Sleep Trainers, Potty Trainers, Walking Consultants, Nutritionists, Lactation Consultants, Speech Therapists, Play Therapists and any other *ist* I could get my hands on.

And The Mothers still insist *they* are right.

I call in tears with my latest crisis—Logan threw sand today; Tabitha is talking back to me; Logan refuses to urinate in one of the 27 receptacles I have purchased for this purpose; Tabitha won't eat what I give her—or anything else for that matter; Logan does not listen to me when I tell him not to do something, even though I told him I *really* wanted him to stop; Tabitha is licking the dog's tongue and won't stop—anything that happens on a daily basis. The Mothers would dish out some form of the same answer:

"That's what kids do."

Sometimes they say something like "Send him to his room if he doesn't listen" or "Maybe she is bored; play with her." I remind them that raising children today is different. These old myths of childrearing are completely ineffective, and what do they know anyway?!? I mean, who did *they* raise? Okay. Maybe that was not my best comeback.

Anyway, I tell them I have to go because I need to consult my library of "How to Raise a Kid" books from people who were FAR more qualified than they to answer. I conclude our call and immerse myself in hours of reading. I talk to the Mommyverse. I call to Dawn and Gigi, and we share war stories. Finally, I call Nate, who needs to be reminded of the lengths I go to to raise his children properly. (He is in a meeting; so I leave him a lengthy voicemail.)

After a period of anguish, I make an appointment with Dr. Godsend. When he enters the exam room, he looks around. Noticing the lack of children with me, he says, "It's just you again."

"I feel the children distract whenever they are here."

"Pediatric appointments can be annoying that way, yes."

I tell him of all the vicious and clearly burgeoning sociopathic behavior of my children. I detail the tireless and extensive research I have done on these matters. I barely make it to the end when I ask what, dear doctor, can possibly be done?

Dr. Godsend crinkles his brow and says, "That's what kids their age do."

Now see, Mothers, THIS is advice I can use!

BONUS!

What to do when you are stuck inside with your kids all day

We have all had those days when we have to keep the kids inside—Rainy Days, smog-alert days, sick days, "They INSIST on wearing that outfit" days, etc. On a few occasions, this "day" turns into "days." Sometimes, around Day Five of ~~imprisonment~~ inside play, you need to rely on your imagination for fun things to do and interesting interactive play.

I thought I would write down some of my ideas that have gone over pretty well in these situations—in case you ever need something to do with the kiddies on an Inside Day.

10 Things to Do With Your Kids on an Inside Day:

1) **"Find the Kids' Favorite TV Program"**—This is one of the easier games. Simply pop the kids in front of the TV; give them bowls of popcorn and chocolate milk; and fire up the remote. To supervise, all you need is a book of your own and something cool to drink. (Rule of thumb; chilled white in the morning, rose for the afternoon and vodka/gin should be reserved for 5:00 o'clock—or about the time the news comes on.) Read your book, and when your children start wrestling or throwing food, just change the channel! It's that easy . . . and you don't even have to look up from your book. There is no reason Suze Ormond can't speak to your little ones—let them do the taxes next year.
Here's the trick: When the channel changes, the kids are so hopeful they will be entertained they are quiet for a good 15 minutes to check out this new show. That should get you well into your next chapter, at least.

2) **Read to your child**—Everyone knows how important reading to a child is. Those little minds are like sponges, thirsting for knowledge. So let them have it. "But how do I keep from cutting my tongue out if I have to see those damn Dogs Go one more time?" you ask? Easy—read to them from YOUR book! You will open up all new worlds to them—ones of time travel and days of yore—times when all women were unquestionably beautiful and men had rippling biceps as well as curly black hair on their structured chests. Teach them about love and how it happens to even the most headstrong daughter of a decent but

wrongly accused patriarch, whose death/reputation said daughter must exonerate.

Let your children know that under even the most bitter man's rock solid chest beats a warm and loving heart that is not known to most. Careful, though. Sometimes the language can get a bit complex. This is where your imagination comes into play. Substitute words for "heaving bosoms" and "succulent nipples" with things like "powder puffs" and "grape popsicles." Fondling and sucking are expected in these incidents. Hardened parts of the male anatomy can be called "rocket ships" that explode into space. The children will be captivated.

Use different voices. Make some of the characters familiar, like referring to the evil stepmother who is trying to do away with the heroine as "Grandma" and the horrid militia trying to lynch the hero as "Tree Hugging, Misguided Liberals." Fun for all.

3) **Have the kids assemble your long-ignored scrapbooks**—They need to get done—your kids need a craft. Load up the table with the thousands of pictures and some glue and anything they can put the pictures in. Not using that Gideon's Bible you stole? Have them pop your wedding photos in Leviticus. *War and Peace* getting you down? The kiddies can turn it into "War and Our First Family Christmas." Who cares if they get the order out of whack—you won't look at them until you are drunk anyway.

4) **Play "What Do I Want To Be When I Grow Up?"**—I write a variety of professions down on sheets of paper and put them in a hat. Then I let the kids pull out the sheets one by one, and they get to act out the profession. I feel very strongly that every lesson should be one that prepares the children for the real world. To do this, I insist the children use real life props and act out the profession as accurately as possible.

Here are the professions we use in our game. Feel free to make up your own: bartender, masseuse who specializes in Mommy's shoulders, person who orders takeout a lot, housecleaner, very quiet person, talk to the telemarketer instead of Mom person and pharmacist.

5) **"What Does That Pill Do?" Game**—This is an offshoot from when my kids practiced pharmacist from the above suggestion. You have your bundles of joy go to the medicine cabinet and pull out anything

in a bottle that has Mommy or Daddy's name on it. Line them up and have them serve you a pill from each bottle—one at a time—and note Mommy's reaction to the pill. Does it make Mommy laugh a lot? That gets labeled the "Happy Pills." Does Mommy go to sleep after she takes the pill? Call that one "Sleep Miser." Does Mommy start smiling and agreeing to let you watch those movies Mommy and Daddy keep on the top shelf while you eat cake frosting from the container—all the while, telling you how much she loves you and calling Daddy to say she loves him too, despite what she said last night?—let's write those down as the "Perfect Pills."

6) **"Where's Mommy?"**—Pretty much hide and seek, but I have made a couple of modifications: I tell the children they must stay perfectly still until the stove timer goes off (set for 15 minutes or more). I mention that, if they do not, that ax wielding creature that inhabits their closet at night will come out and find them.

Also, I can suggest a few places you had not thought of: a) the crawl space above or below your house, the one you cannot access without a key or ladder. b) the neighbors' patio if it is fully shielded from your yard and they are not home. c) the mall. And, lastly, d), the floor of their room—since they cannot see the toys or clothes there, how will they see you?

7) **"List the Reasons Daddy Does Not Deserve Mommy As He Sits In His Air-Conditioned Office With No Children"**—This one takes a bit more effort on your part as the children tend to need a lot of help with the reasons. After you have carefully listed them out (you may need to write the reasons yourself), have the kids decorate the sheets with stamps and banana peel stickers and the jam stuck to the table from lunch (be very careful that they do not mar the reasons in any way that they cannot be read) and present them to Daddy when he walks in the door after work. If Daddy is late for any reason, have the children throw the sheets at him, possibly anchored with the empty bottle of wine you just polished off.

8) **"Try to Guess Why Mommy Won't Stop Crying?"**—Simple guessing game. Be careful, as the children throw out answers, if you can hear them over your uncontrollable sobs, you may be reminded of a few things you hadn't thought of since breakfast. Leave plenty of time for this game.

9) **"Let's See How Many Websites We Can Visit Until The Credit Card Company Calls Mommy—Again"**—All kids should know their way around the internet, and a little lesson in commerce serves everyone in life. Bookmark a few of your favorite sites, and let the kids at the mouse. Teach them how to match the numbers on the plastic rectangle in their hands to the little box on the screen.

As always when your children are on the internet, they should be heavily supervised. If you are not there to watch over them, you may end up with a yard full of plastic balls instead of this season's scrunch boots; so make sure your glass is full before you sit down—it takes just a minute for a kid to find their way to the Toys R Us website.

10) Lastly, if you absolutely cannot think of another way to preserve your sanity and your children's lives for one more second, break out the *Fun for Kids* craft books. In there, you will find hundreds upon hundreds of exciting and colorful ideas for crafts and projects that better not only their minds but their hearts. Rip the pages out one by one, ball them up and throw them at the dog. He gets his run for the day, and you and the kids work out your throwing arm.

Take your wine glass, and dump its contents on to a series of pages (don't worry—most liquor stores deliver). Have the kids shred up the pieces and put the freshly minted papyrus in Daddy's slack's pockets—a surprise for later—made with "love." Take some of the wine-soaked paper and teach your kids about spitballs—this should give them a leg up for school. Line up all the photos of near and distant relatives and have some target practice.

What's left, light on fire (might want to have a pitcher of water handy. Best fill it with the stuff from the sink—it is weird how the box of Gallo and the Brita look alike after five days inside with the kids). This should teach the kids something about science or nature or homeowners' insurance—what does it matter? The Weatherman just came on and told you to expect to stay inside again tomorrow.

Glossary of Terms

SWOC—Single WithOut Children

SAHM—Stay At Home Mother

Mommyverse—the universe of Moms through internet, books, television, support groups and any other form of media that reaches a mom's life

The Mothers—the combination of Mother and Mother-in-Law, who elect themselves judge and jury

Acknowledgements

The majority of this book is fiction. I have borrowed from actual events and pieces of people but the folks mentioned are figments of my imagination and not anyone in my life.

Really.

Specifically: I have both a mother and a mother in law. They are each very bright and accomplished women. They stayed home to raise their children after which they went on to successful careers. They do not offer advice about my household or children unless I expressly ask them.

I am grateful to my mother in law for all of her insight and to my mother who really is the greatest resource I have in all aspects of life, but especially mothering. And is, in fact, always right.

My best friend, Elizabeth is always at the other end of the phone to make me laugh or let me cry.

My husband Scott encourages everything I do. Even write books that make fun of husbands.

I am indebted to Scott, Dad, Mom, Ted Mills, Matt Ragghianti and Margie Wells who served as editors.

I want to mention my brothers here because they appear nowhere in the book. However they are really great brothers and I may not ever write another book so I want to say this now.

Lastly there is my father. He gets really angry that dads never get thanked. You were a great dad and I love you very much and thank you. But we both know that Mom did all the work.